The last, hazy days of August are meant for basking in the sun and reading good books. Whether you're relaxing in your backyard, on your porch or maybe chilling on vacation, make sure to have a selection of Harlequin Presents titles by your side. We've got eight great novels to choose from….

Bestselling author Lynne Graham presents her latest tale of a mistress who's forced to marry an Italian billionaire in *Mistress Bought and Paid For*. And Miranda Lee is as steamy as ever with her long-awaited romp, *Love-Slave to the Sheikh*, for our hot UNCUT miniseries.

You never know what goes on behind closed doors, and we have three very different stories about marriages to prove it: Anne Mather's sexy and emotional *Jack Riordan's Baby* will have your heart in your mouth while also tugging at its strings, while *Bought by Her Husband*, Sharon Kendrick's newest release, and Kate Walker's *The Antonakos Marriage* are two slices of Greek tycoon heaven with spicy twists!

If it's something more traditional you're after, we've plenty of choice: *By Royal Demand*, the first installment in Robyn Donald's new regal saga, THE ROYAL HOUSE OF ILLYRIA, won't disappoint. Or you might like to try *The Italian Millionaire's Virgin Wife* by Diana Hamilton and *His Very Personal Assistant* by Carole Mortimer—two shy, sensible, prim-and-proper women find themselves living lives they've never dreamed of when they attract two rich, arrogant and darkly handsome men!

Enjoy!

Harlequin Presents®

UNCUT

More passion for your reading pleasure!

Escape into a world of intense passion and scorching romance! You'll find the drama, the emotion, the international settings and happy endings that you've always loved in Harlequin Presents® books. But we've turned up the thermostat just a little, so that the relationships really sizzle. Careful, they're almost too hot to handle!

Look for some of your favorite bestselling authors in Presents®

UNCUT titles!

Miranda Lee
Love-Slave to the Sheikh

uNcut

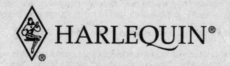

HARLEQUIN®

TORONTO • NEW YORK • LONDON
AMSTERDAM • PARIS • SYDNEY • HAMBURG
STOCKHOLM • ATHENS • TOKYO • MILAN • MADRID
PRAGUE • WARSAW • BUDAPEST • AUCKLAND

ISBN-13: 978-0-373-12556-2
ISBN-10:   0-373-12556-9

LOVE-SLAVE TO THE SHEIKH

First North American Publication 2006.

Copyright © 2006 by Miranda Lee.

Printed in U.S.A.

All about the author...
Miranda Lee

MIRANDA LEE was born in Port Macquarie, a popular seaside town on the mid-north coast of New South Wales, Australia. Her father was a country schoolteacher and brilliant sportsman. Her mother was a talented dressmaker.

After leaving her convent school, Miranda briefly studied the cello before moving to Sydney, where she embraced the emerging world of computers. Her career as a programmer ended after she married, had three daughters and bought a small acreage in a semirural community.

Miranda attempted greyhound training, as well as horse and goat breeding, but was left dissatisfied. She yearned to find a creative career from which she could earn money. When her sister suggested writing romances, it seemed like a good idea. She could do it at home, and it might even be fun!

It took a decade of trial and error before her first romance, *After the Affair,* was accepted and published. At that time, Miranda, her husband and her three daughters had moved back to the central coast, where they could enjoy the sun and the surf lifestyle once again.

Numerous successful stories followed, each embodying Miranda's trademark style: fast-paced and sexy rhythms; passionate, real-life characters; and enduring, memorable story lines. She has one credo when writing romances: Don't bore the reader! Millions of fans worldwide agree she never does.

PROLOGUE

'You do not need to couch your diagnosis in soft terms. Please tell me the reality of my situation.'

The neurosurgeon looked across his desk at his VIP patient. He did not doubt that Sheikh Bandar bin Saeed al Serkel meant his brave words. But he wondered if the Sheikh was really prepared to hear that his odds of surviving were the same as those the bookmakers were giving on the Sheikh's three-year-old colt winning the Derby?

Even money.

'You have a brain tumour,' the doctor told him. 'It is malignant,' he added, impressed when the dark eyes fixed on him did not flinch or even flicker.

People usually paled at such news. But this man was holding strong. Maybe it was the Arab way—their belief that their lives belonged to Allah. Maybe he was thinking that if it was Allah's will that he die, then so be it.

Yet the man was only thirty-four years old. To all outward intents and purposes he was a splendid physical specimen of manhood. No one would guess by looking at him that he had cancer. Or, for that matter, that he was a sheikh.

Not for him any form of Arab dress. Or facial hair. His tall, lean body was clothed in the best Savile Row suit. His long, leanly handsome face was clean shaven.

But a sheikh he was. The only son of an oil-rich zillionaire and a London socialite—both of whom had been tragically killed in a fire on board a luxury yacht—he was Oxford-educated and currently lived in England, where he owned an apartment in Kensington, a stable full of expensive racehorses at Newmarket, and a stud farm in Wales.

The doctor's impressed secretary had made it her business to discover all there was to know about her employer's most exotic and possibly most wealthy patient. She'd been going on about him for a whole week, especially about his playboy reputation. He not only owned fast horses, he drove fast cars and dated fast women. Fast and very beautiful women.

The surgeon hadn't been impressed. Till now.

'And?' the Sheikh prompted.

The surgeon gathered himself to deliver the final blow. 'If you do not have surgery you will be dead within a year. The surgery, however, is risky. Your chances of survival are about fifty-fifty. The decision is yours,' he finished, with a shrug of his shoulders.

The Sheikh smiled, his flashing teeth looking extra white against his olive skin.

'You make it sound like I have a choice in the matter. If I do nothing, I will surely die. So of course you must operate. Are you the best man for this job?'

The doctor drew himself up in his chair, his shoulders broadening. 'I am the best there is in the United Kingdom.'

The Sheikh nodded, his striking face serious once more. 'I have great faith in the British. They do not overestimate their abilities as some people do. And they are excellent under pressure. Schedule surgery for me for the last week in June.'

'But that's three weeks away. I would prefer to operate as soon as possible.'

'Will my chances of survival be much worse by waiting three weeks?'

The surgeon frowned. It was never good to wait with cancer. 'Possibly not a great deal worse,' he conceded. 'Still, I do not recommend it.'

This time the Sheikh's smile was wry. 'But I am assured of staying alive for at least those three weeks, am I not?'

'Your headaches will get worse.'

'Can you give me something for them?'

The surgeon sighed. 'I'll write you a prescription,' he agreed grudgingly. 'But I am still not happy about this delay. What is your reason for waiting that long?'

'I must go to Australia.'

'Australia! What on earth for?'

'Prince Ali of Dubar has asked me to look after his thoroughbred stud farm there whilst he goes home for his brother's coronation. You might have read that King Khaled passed away yesterday?'

The doctor hadn't. He avoided reading the news. When he wasn't working he preferred to do something relaxing, like play chess. But he knew where Dubar was, and how wealthy its royal family were.

'Surely Prince Ali could get someone else?'

'I must grant my good friend's request. Ali saved my life once when we were boys and has never asked anything of me in return. I cannot deny him this favour.'

'But if you told him of your medical condition…?'

'My medical condition is my own private and personal matter. I and I alone will deal with it.'

'You need the support of friends and family at a time like this.'

For the first time those dark eyes betrayed something. A moment of weakness. No, of bleakness.

'I have no family,' he stated brusquely.

'But you do have friends. This Prince Ali, for instance. You should tell him about the tumour.'

'Not till he returns to Australia from his commitments in Dubar.' The Arab stood up abruptly. 'Your secretary has my e-mail address. Have her send me the hospital arrangements. Till then…' He held his hand out across the desk.

The surgeon stood up and shook it. Such a strong hand. Such a strong man. He would do his best to save the Sheikh. But he could not perform miracles.

'Look after yourself,' he advised.

'Can I ride?'

The query startled the doctor. This was the first patient awaiting delicate brain surgery who'd asked him such a question. Usually they wrapped themselves in cotton wool. They didn't fly off to Australia and ride horses and do goodness knew what else.

Still, to be honest, riding horses was unlikely to kill the man. Unless he fell off and broke his neck. He had a tumour, not an aneurism.

'I suppose you can,' he said. 'If you must.'

The Sheikh smiled again. An enigmatic smile this time.

'I must.'

CHAPTER ONE

'WHAT a total waste of time,' Samantha muttered as she threw her bag onto the back seat of her four-wheel drive, then slammed the door shut.

'And a total waste of money,' she added to herself, after she'd climbed in behind the wheel and started the engine.

Her only consolation was that she didn't have a too-long drive in front of her. The distance from Williamstown airport to the upper Hunter Valley was considerably less than the journey from Sydney airport. Only a one-and-a-half-hour trip as opposed to at least three.

Still, as Samantha angled the vehicle out of the car park and headed for the highway, her sigh carried frustration and disappointment. She should never have listened to Cleo. A five-day package holiday at a Gold Coast resort—regardless of how hip-hopping the place was—had never been going to find her a boyfriend, either long term or short term.

The wildly romantic notion of meeting the love of her life at such a place was just that: a wildly romantic notion.

The possibility of having a holiday fling hadn't been

high on the chance meter, either. Samantha just wasn't the
sort of girl to pick up some handsome hunk who'd treat
her to a few nights of wining and dining, followed by the
kind of sex women dreamt about but rarely enjoyed.

Oh, she was presentable enough to attract some male
attention these days, especially after Cleo had dragged her
off last week to a beauty salon in Newcastle to have her
long mid-brown hair streaked blonde and her naturally
thick eyebrows plucked into elegantly slender arches.
It had also helped that she now owned a few attention-
grabbing outfits which made the most of her tall, athletic
figure; Cleo had taken her clothes-shopping as well.

Samantha had to admit she'd looked pretty good
these past five days.

Several guys had approached her, both around the
pool and at the restaurant bar every evening.

It was her manner, she knew, which had quickly
put them off.

She'd never mastered the art of flirting. Or of idle
chit-chat. Or of sucking up to male egos.

Over the years she'd been constantly told by her
girlfriends that she was too blunt. Too opinionated.
Too assertive.

The truth was she didn't know how to act all girlie.
She'd never learned, never had a feminine role model
during her formative years.

Samantha had grown up in an all-male household,
with four brothers who'd taught her how to be one of
the boys. She'd learned to play sport like a boy and stick
up for herself like a boy—with her fists. She'd never
learned to defer to the male sex. Oh, no. If she'd done
that in the Nelson home she'd have spent all her days

in tears, trodden into the ground by her highly competitive, testosterone-fuelled brothers.

So she'd competed with them, and often beat them.

Not smart, her girlfriends at school had often told her. Definitely not smart.

Samantha had come to agree by the time she graduated. She hadn't had a single date during her high school years, let alone a steady boyfriend. She'd had to be escorted to her graduation ball by one of her brothers.

Admittedly, back then she'd been rather gawky-looking. Very tall and skinny, with no bust to speak of. Her extra short hairdo hadn't helped, either. Neither had her lack of flair with clothes and make-up.

By the time Samantha had entered Sydney University to do a veterinary science degree she'd just about given up on getting herself a boyfriend. Her love of animals—horses in particular—had filled the empty space in her heart. She'd paid for her higher education by working as a stablehand at a nearby racing stables.

University, however, Samantha had soon discovered, had a different code of sexual behaviour from the rest of the world. Not too many girls—even the plain, nerdy ones—finished their degrees as virgins. Most of the male students treated sex as a challenge and a sport. The more notches on their belt, the better. They didn't much care what their conquests looked like, or how they acted.

Samantha had eventually supplied a couple of notches during her four-year stint at uni. She'd grown her hair long during that time, developed some breasts, and had actually begun to look more like a girl.

But neither of her experiences—both of which had

been disappointingly brief—had rivalled the earth-moving events she'd read about in books. Love had certainly eluded her.

After graduating from university she'd gone to work for a vet at Randwick who specialised in the treatment of racehorses. He'd been in his early forties, a nice-looking, charming man who was very married.

In the beginning there had been no attraction between them. But after a couple of years their long hours of working together and their mutual passion for horses had created an intimacy between them. They'd formed a friendship which Samantha had found both fulfilling and flattering. She still hadn't been having any success with the opposite sex—perhaps she shouldn't have stayed living at home—so it had been very nice to have a man enjoy her company. Very nice, too, to have her natural intelligence and strong opinions appreciated and not put down.

She hadn't fallen in love with Paul. But she had come to look forward to the time they spent together. He'd made her feel good. She had become only too ready to work increasingly long hours, and to accept his invitations for more cups of coffee than was perhaps wise.

A more sophisticated girl would have seen it coming, the evening when Paul had grabbed her and pulled her into his arms and kissed her. His declaration of love had been quite thrilling. Samantha hadn't heard such passionate words before. Not directed at her, anyway.

For one awful moment she'd been tempted to give in to that voice which said that maybe this man's love was all she would ever have. She'd been nearly twenty-five, still dateless and almost desperate. But at the last second she'd looked over Paul's shoulder and glimpsed the photo of his wife and children which he kept on his desk, and she'd instinctively known he wasn't about to leave them. She'd suspected that what he wanted from her was not love, but the excitement of an extra-marital affair. A very convenient one at that.

Only the previous weekend Samantha had seen a programme on television which had interviewed a series of 'other women'. Sam had been amazed to find that they weren't *femme fatale* types, but mostly women with poor self-esteem, ones who were willing to accept the crumbs from their married lovers' tables. Most seemed not to believe they would ever find that one special person who was free to love them as they deserved to be loved.

Samantha didn't want second best. She'd never settled for second best in any other area of her life. Why should she with love? She wanted a man who didn't belong to some other woman. She wanted her own man, one who could give her everything she secretly desired. His undying love. His ring on her finger. And his children.

So she'd left her job with Paul. Left Sydney and home as well, after applying for—and to her surprise securing—an advertised position to be a live-in vet at the Dubar Royal Stud Farm.

An avid racing fan, Samantha had already known this highly regarded stud was one of the biggest and best breeding establishments in Australia. Run by an extremely wealthy Arab prince, money was never any object: they had the best stallions standing there—some flown in for the Australian season from other parts of the world—they had the best broodmares money could buy, and presumably the best equine practitioners tending them.

Given her rather limited experience with the breeding side of racehorses, Samantha had been surprised when she'd got the job. Still, she was a quick learner, and she'd soon learned all she needed to know from the other live-in vet—a very overweight man in his late fifties named Gerald.

To be honest, however, Samantha wasn't sure that it was what she wanted to do for the rest of her life. At the time of accepting the position she'd just wanted to get away from the temptation of Paul.

Of course there'd also been the added lure of a country lifestyle. She'd hoped that maybe country men wouldn't be as picky as city guys. Maybe they wouldn't find her blunt manner quite so off-putting. Or her choice of career in any way odd. Surely they wouldn't mind her preference for a low-maintenance look most of the time? Country women weren't renowned for wearing scads of make-up or always appearing as if they'd just stepped out of the hairdressers.

Samantha sighed as she steered her four-by-four down the wide main street of yet another small country town.

Unfortunately, her personal life at the Dubar Royal Stud hadn't worked out much differently than it had back in Sydney. The truth was she intimidated country guys even more than city guys. Most of the younger men working at the stud hardly dared look at her, let alone speak to her. Only Jack, who was a sweetie but somewhat on the slow side, seemed to be able to deal with her.

Ali, of course, spoke to her, but frankly Samantha found *him* intimidating. His wife, too. The stunningly beautiful Charmaine was an ex-supermodel who spent quite a bit of time doing charity work in Sydney. They had two children, a darling little girl named Amanda and a boy, Bandar, who was one year old, and named after some life-long friend of the Prince's—an oil-rich, racehorse-owning sheikh who lived in London and had an even worse reputation with women than Ali had before he'd got married a few years back.

Samantha only knew all this because Cleo had told her. As the Prince's housekeeper, and part-time nanny to his children, Cleo was in a position to know quite a lot about the Prince and his family. She wasn't a malicious gossip—in fact she was a lovely lady—but she did like to talk. During the occasions when Ali and his family went to Sydney for the weekend Cleo would invite Samantha up to the main house for dinner and a board game afterwards, during which the two women would chat away about anything and everything. They'd got along really well right from the first day, despite Cleo being around fifty.

If it hadn't been for Cleo's bright company Samantha would have cut and run before. As it was, she knew she wouldn't be renewing her contract when it ran out at the end of June. The truth was she missed Sydney and city life. The peace and quiet of the countryside was very nice in theory, but Samantha found it far too lonely up here.

That was why she'd been so susceptible to Cleo's suggestion about the Gold Coast getaway. She'd been due some time off. But truly she should have known it would be a foolish and futile waste of time.

Still, at least going there had achieved one thing. It had made Samantha realise she *could* attract a man—physically. Cleo's makeover had worked wonders in that regard. What she needed to learn now was how to play the dating—and mating—game, *after* the initial contact had been made. Samantha wasn't sure exactly how she was going to learn this, or who would be best to teach her, but she knew if she was serious about getting married she simply would have to change.

As she drove along the highway on autopilot—her preoccupied mind not taking any notice of her surrounds—Samantha began to wonder if there were businesses in Sydney who ran that kind of course. What she needed, she decided, was a flirting coach, who gave lessons in what to say and how to act.

A few lessons in lovemaking might not be a bad idea, either! But she supposed there weren't too many of those schools around. Or teachers. What a pity the two guys she'd slept with at uni had been clueless. What she needed to find was an older man who only wanted her for one thing and knew a thing or two about sex.

An *unmarried* older man, she reminded herself when Paul's face jumped into her head.

'Darn it!' Samantha exclaimed when she realised she'd driven right past the entrance to the stud.

Braking, she pulled over to the side of the road, and the semi-trailer which had been tailgating her practically took her side window off as it roared past.

'Cowboy!' she yelled at him out of the window.

She took her time making a U-turn, her eyes scanning the nearby paddocks as she did so.

'Mmm. Must have rained while I was away,' she remarked aloud. There was a touch of green about them. At this time of year the frosts had usually browned the grass right off, and the horses were mainly hand fed.

Not that they needed rain. Unlike other parts of Australia, the Hunter Valley rarely seemed to be affected by drought. The land was rich and fertile, flat along the riverbanks, then gently undulating as the land rose towards the Great Dividing Range. Perfect for growing crops and raising thoroughbreds.

Samantha turned into the wide gravel driveway, stopping in front of the huge black iron gates which were as impressive as every part of the property. The Dubar royal insignia was built into the middle of both gates, outlined in gold to stand out against the black.

Samantha zapped the gates open with the remote control she'd been given when she started work here. As she drove through, she recalled how awed she'd been by this place that first day. The no-expense-spared budget was obvious, from the freshly painted white wooden fences which enclosed each horse paddock to the magnificently modern barns and stables.

But it was the main residence which drew the eye as you drove up the long, wide, grey gravel driveway. A huge white-stuccoed, single-storeyed building, the house stretched across the top of a hill, its position giving it the perfect view of the valley below.

Samantha thought it looked like an abbey from an ancient land, with its many Moroccan style archways and cloistered verandahs. It certainly didn't look like an Australian farmhouse.

But of course it wasn't an Australian farmhouse. It

was a mansion fit for a prince. An Arab prince, rich beyond most people's wildest dreams.

A hundred metres or so below and to the left of the house was a smaller hilltop which had been levelled to make way for a helipad, from which Ali would fly to Sydney every weekend. His private and personal helicopter was huge and black. An ex-army aircraft, the interior had been fitted out with every luxury and security device. Or so she'd been told by Cleo.

Samantha had never actually been in it.

The helicopter was sitting on the helipad now, its dark silhouette faintly ominous against the clear blue sky.

Samantha wondered momentarily what it was doing there on a Monday. Usually Ali sent it straight back to Sydney after he returned on a Sunday evening. Despite his wealth, he did not keep the helicopter here all the time: it, and its pilot, stayed in Sydney all week, so they could be available for charter and mercy flights.

No doubt she'd find out the reason for its presence when she spoke to Cleo. That woman knew everything about everyone around here. Samantha would give her a ring once she'd unpacked her things and had a cup of coffee. Which reminded her. She'd better turn her mobile phone back on once she reached the cottage. Her five-day retreat from real life was over.

The driveway forked after a while, the short straight road on the left leading to the stallion quarters and the breeding barn, the winding road on the right heading uphill to the helipad and the house. Samantha took the track in the middle, which followed the river and would eventually take her to the cottage where she lived.

The river flats were given mostly to growing feed for

the horses, oats and lucerne. Though not in the winter. It was also the site of the training track where the yearlings were broken in, and where some of the older racehorses were given light work after spelling on the property—the aim being to get some of the fat off them before they were sent back to their city stables.

As Samantha approached the training track, she frowned at a most unusual sight, slowing her speed to a crawl as she drove past. There was a horse on the track—odd for this time of day. The clock on the dash showed just after noon. It was a big grey horse, its bridle being held by a tall, dark-haired man wearing hip-hugging blue jeans and an open-necked white shirt with long, fullish sleeves.

Samantha didn't recognise the man, but she sure recognised the horse. Smoking Gun was a highly prized stallion, flown over from England to stand here at stud this year at some phenomenal service fee. He had arrived a couple of weeks ago, to rest up after his first season in the Northern Hemisphere. His owner was the playboy Sheikh after whom Ali's son had been named: Bandar. Ali had warned all the staff before the horse's arrival that they were to protect the Sheikh's horse with their lives.

The stallion had not settled all that well, and it required a lot of time in the exercise yard to stop him kicking holes in the walls of his stable. They'd moved him into a specially padded stall to prevent injury, but by the end of last week there'd been talk of sending for a particular groom back in England who was famous for handling difficult stallions. A gypsy, according to Cleo.

Samantha presumed that was who was launching

himself into the saddle at the moment. The man certainly looked like a gypsy, with his black collar-length hair and deeply olive skin.

Sam's stomach tightened when the stallion reared, then danced around in circles, fighting for his head. One part of her brain could see that a long, steady gallop around the track might be more settling than a short romp around an exercise yard. But what if the horse started racing at full speed? What if he broke a bone? The stallion was carrying a lot more weight than during his racing days. What if something unexpected happened, like a dog running onto the track or something? Smoking Gun might stumble, or veer off and run into the fence.

Samantha glanced worriedly around. There was no one else in sight. No one watching. Not a single soul.

That was even more odd.

Alarm bells began ringing in her head. Ali would not have sanctioned this idea, no matter how unsettled Smoking Gun had become. It suddenly became clear that this groom—this gypsy!—had taken it upon himself to do this without permission.

She had to stop him.

Jamming on the brakes, she was out of her vehicle in a flash. But before she could shout a warning, the gypsy gave the stallion his head. The grey took off, its mane and tail streaming back. By the time Samantha leapt up onto the fence the horse and rider were almost at the first corner of the track, the grey's big hooves sending up clouds of dust.

Sam's heart remained in her mouth as they thundered down the back straight. Too late to do anything now. If she started waving her arms around, or ran out onto the track in an attempt to stop them, she might cause the kind of accident she feared. She would have to wait till this idiot decided Smoking Gun had had enough exercise.

Then she would tell him what she thought of him.

Her blood began to boil when he completed not one, but three circuits of the track. The stallion's grey flanks were spotted with foam by the time the rider reined him in, not all that far from where Samantha was now gripping the top railing of the fence with white-knuckled fury.

'What in heaven's name did you think you were doing?' she threw at him, her voice literally shaking. 'Did you ask Prince Ali's permission to exercise Smoking Gun in such a reckless fashion?'

The rider trotted the sweating stallion over towards her.

'And who might you be?' he shot back at her in an upper-crust English accent. Far too upper-crust for a gypsy groom.

Unfortunately, when Samantha's temper was on the boil she had a tendency not to be too observant.

It was impossible, however, not to feel the impact of the man's sex appeal. For a split second she just stared at him. What eyes he had! And what skin! His body wasn't half bad, either.

Her momentary weakness annoyed her all the more.

'I'm Samantha Nelson,' she snapped. 'One of the resident vets here. I presume you're the supposedly expert horseman sent out from England? Look, I'm not saying you don't ride extremely well, but what you did just now was foolhardy. So I repeat: did you have the Prince's permission?'

'I did not,' he replied, his tone and manner so impossibly haughty that it took Samantha's breath away. 'I do not need his permission,' he added, then actually tossed his head at her, as if he was king of the castle and she the dirty rascal.

It finally sank into Samantha's momentarily addled brain that the man she was trying to tear strips off just might not be a groom, let alone a gypsy.

Her stomach contracted as she realised his looks were not dissimilar from Prince Ali's, though he wasn't quite as traditionally handsome as her employer. This man's face was longer and leaner, his cheekbones harder, his mouth the only soft thing about his face.

Yet she found him far more attractive than Ali. He was as spirited as the horse beneath him—which, even now, wouldn't stand still.

'Ali has returned to Dubar for his brother's coronation,' the Arab informed her, his right hand tugging sharply at the bridle before reaching up to rake his hair back from where it had fallen across his face. 'Ali has put me in charge here till his return.'

Samantha found herself floundering under this unexpected turn of events. Or was it this man's overwhelmingly disturbing presence which was causing her normally sharp brain to lose focus? Finally, she gathered herself enough to absorb the facts behind his news. Ali's father, the King of Dubar, must have died whilst she'd been away. Samantha also reasoned that this man could not possibly be a close relative—or one of the royal family—or he'd be back in Dubar as well.

He might be an Arab, but underneath his autocratic manner he was just another employee, like herself. A man too big for his boots in more ways than one. Samantha couldn't seem to help finding him physically attractive, but she didn't like him. And she wasn't about to let him ride roughshod over her.

'Well, perhaps he should have put someone with more sense in charge!'

His black eyes bored into her, his very elegant nostrils flaring in shock. 'You are a very impertinent woman.'

'So I have been told on countless occasions,' she countered, with a defiant head toss of her own newly streaked blonde hair. Samantha supposed he wasn't used to a woman challenging him, which made her want to challenge him all the more. 'But I meant what I said. What you did with that horse was reckless in the extreme. Just look at him. He's exhausted.' At last Smoking Gun had calmed down, and was standing sedately beneath his irritatingly cool rider.

The Arab cocked a dark brow at her. 'That was precisely the point. He needed an outlet for his testosterone. He's become used to servicing several mares a day. He's young, and has yet to adjust to his life at stud. He wants what he wants when he wants it—like most young male animals. In time, he will learn that all good things come to those who wait.'

'Maybe so. But you can hardly ride him like that every day till he learns to control his urges. Or till the next season starts. It's way too risky.'

'*I* will assess the risk, madam. Not you.'

'Put him in a larger exercise yard, if you must. Riding him full bore on this track, however, is out of the question. I'm sure Prince Ali would not approve.'

'Whether or not Prince Ali approves is immaterial to me.'

Samantha fumed some more. The arrogance of this man was unbelievable. 'I will contact the Prince,' she threatened, 'and tell him what you're doing.'

The Arab actually laughed at her. 'Do that, madam. Ali won't tell me to stop. Smoking Gun belongs to *me*. I own every inch of this horse and I can ride him to death if I want to. I might contact Ali about *you*, however. I might tell him that his lady vet is as foolish as she is fearless. No, no—do not argue with me any longer. The horse is tired, and so am I. You can argue with me over dinner tonight. Eight o'clock. Do not keep me waiting. My time is precious to me.'

With that, he whirled and trotted the weary horse to the track exit, not giving Samantha a backward glance as he headed back towards the stallion barn.

CHAPTER TWO

FOR the first time in her life, Samantha was left speechless by a man.

It took her a full minute to gather herself enough to make it back to the four-by-four, her normally excellent co-ordination in total tatters as she fumbled with the door handle, then banged her shin on her way up behind the wheel. Pride demanded she not look in the rear vision mirror, but her pride was in tatters too, it seemed. She sat there for simply ages, staring in the mirror, till Smoking Gun and his playboy sheikh owner were mere dots in the distance.

Only then did she pull her fatuous gaze away, telling herself it was surprise and nothing more which had robbed her of her usual composure.

Samantha began to fume once more during the short drive home. Who did this Bandar think he was, ordering her around like that? He might own Smoking Gun, but he didn't own *her*! He wasn't even her employer. Her contract was with Prince Ali, not him. She didn't have to have dinner with him if she didn't want to.

The trouble was, Samantha realised with considerable chagrin as she pulled up in front of the tiny weatherboard cottage which she currently called home, she *did* want to.

The female in her—that part which could not deny he was the sexiest man she'd ever met—wanted to spend more time with him, wanted to look at him some more, wanted to argue with him some more.

Their encounter had left her angry, yes. But excited, too. Excited in a way she'd never experienced before. All her senses seemed heightened. Her skin tingled at the thought of being in his presence again, of having those gorgeous eyes on her once more.

A quiver ran down her spine at the memory of them, and the way they had looked at her.

Had he found *her* attractive? Dared she hope he'd invited her to dinner because she interested him as a woman?

A quick glance in the side mirror put paid to that little fantasy. It was a passable face these days. Having her eyebrows plucked had really opened up her eyes. But she wasn't about to grace the cover of any women's magazines just yet. Her chin was too square, her mouth too wide and her neck too long. She did have good teeth, though. She'd have passed muster if she'd been a horse.

'Heavens to Betsy!' she exclaimed irritatedly as she propelled herself out of the four-wheel drive. 'No wonder he called me foolish. I *am* a fool for ever thinking a man like that would fancy someone like me.'

Slamming the driver's door, she yanked open the back door and hauled out her bag. Everyone who'd ever read a gossip magazine knew that billionaire Arab sheikhs dated supermodels and socialites. Sometimes they even married them. You only had to look at Ali's beautiful blonde wife to see the type they went for.

Samantha had her job cut out for her attracting an ordinary guy. The Sheikh was way out of her league in more ways than one.

'Not that I really care,' she grumbled as she marched up the steps which led onto the rather rickety front verandah. 'The man's obviously a male chauvinist pig of the first order.'

She just wished he hadn't called her fearless. Wished those incredible eyes of his hadn't flashed at her as he'd said the word. There'd been admiration in that flash.

Or had it been amusement?

Samantha's top lip curled at this last thought. She didn't like the idea of being invited to dinner to amuse the Sheikh. But why else would he have invited her?

Her perverse mind—or was it her unquashable ego?—catapulted her back to the flattering notion that he just might have fancied her.

The chilly air inside the cottage swiftly brought Samantha back to reality. *And* the present. Lighting the combustion heater would have to take priority over indulging in more wildly romantic fantasies.

But by the time she'd walked into the front bedroom and dropped her bag by the bed, Samantha found herself wanting to hurry over to open the old wardrobe and take another look at herself—this time in the full-length mirror which hung on the back of the door.

Taking off her leather jacket, she tried to see herself as a man might see her, doing her level best to ignore her own preconceived ideas about herself. Her gaze started at the top, then worked slowly downwards. She turned sidewards, checking herself in profile, and then her bejeaned rear view, before remembering that the Sheikh hadn't seen her from behind.

Pity. She had a good rear view—especially in stretch jeans.

After five minutes, Samantha had a much more positive checklist about her overall appearance than the quick one she'd made back in the car.

Face. Not bad. Nice blue eyes. Clear skin. Great teeth.

Hair. Good. No, better than good. Sexy. She now had sexy hair, when it was out. Which it was at the moment.

Figure. Damned good. Provided a man didn't mind tall, with B-cup breasts. But she had great legs, a flat stomach and a tight butt.

Who knew? Maybe the Sheikh had grown bored with all his super-glamorous, super-sucking-up girl-friends and wanted to try something different. Like a six-foot-tall Aussie girl with an attitude problem and a suddenly over-inflated opinion of herself.

'Truly, you've begun to let Cleo's mini makeover go to your head,' Samantha muttered.

That's what I should do, Samantha decided sensibly after shutting the wardrobe door. Ring Cleo and find out exactly what's going on around here.

Samantha scooped her bag up off the floor, dumped it onto the plain white duvet which covered the double bed and unzipped one of the side pockets. Extracting her mobile phone, she turned it back on, ignoring the message bank ringtone which heralded missed messages, and called the number up at the main house.

'Norm, here. How can I help you?'

Samantha was momentarily taken aback. Norm was Cleo's husband. He worked for Prince Ali as well, as a general handyman and gardener around the house. But he never answered the phone.

'Norm?' she said. 'Hi. It's Samantha. Is Cleo there?'

'Hi, there, love. Yep, she's here—running around like a chook with her head cut off. You've no idea what's happened.'

'Er…what?' Samantha thought it best not to tell Norm about her run-in with the Sheikh.

'Ali's dad kicked the bucket last Thursday—the day after you left—and Ali's had to go home for the funeral, plus his brother's coronation. The whole family's gone for three weeks. Anyway, Ali asked this mate of his to keep an eye on the place whilst he's gone. He's the bloke they named little Bandar after: Sheikh Bandar bin Something-or-other. Cleo knows all about him. You can ask her later. Anyway, we thought he wasn't arriving here till tomorrow. He flew in from London last night and was supposed to rest up today in that hotel suite in Sydney that Ali owns. But it seems he was keen to get here and see to that horse of his. You know the one. He's been giving poor Ray a whole heap of trouble.'

Samantha knew the one all right. But he wouldn't be giving the stallion manager so much trouble after his three-mile gallop around the track today.

'Anyway, Cleo was a bit upset, because she didn't have the main guest suite ready for him,' Norm raved on, 'so that's what she's been doing. It's Samantha, love!' he called out, presumably to his wife. 'Yes, she's back. You are back, aren't you?' he directed at Samantha.

'Yes. I'm back.'

'She's back! Here's Cleo. She wants to talk to you.'

'Samantha. Why are you back so early? You weren't due home till late this afternoon.'

'I caught an earlier flight.'

'Oh-oh. That doesn't sound like the Gold Coast trip was a raging success.'

'It was a nice break.'

'You didn't get lucky, then?'

'Nope.'

'Never mind. It was worth a try. Did Norm tell you what's been going on here?'

'He sure did. Poor Ali. Was he upset about his dad dying?'

'Hardly. The old man had him exiled, after all. But he was glad for his brother. Said it was about time Dubar had a king who was more in touch with the real world. Have you heard about our very interesting temporary visitor?'

'Yep. Norm told me. Though he couldn't quite remember all his names. Only the Sheikh Bandar bit.'

Cleo laughed. 'Yes, I can't remember all his names, either. But he's a bit like Ali where names are concerned. Doesn't stand on too much ceremony. Likes to be called Bandar.'

'Really?'

'Yes, really. Doesn't let grass grow under his feet, either. Was off to see his horse as soon as he arrived. But not before asking me to put on a small dinner party tonight. Nothing grand, he said. He just wants a getting-to-know-everyone meal with the main management staff. I presume he means Ray and Trevor. Gerald, too, of course—which means you'll probably get an invitation as well.'

'He's already asked me,' Samantha confessed, feeling foolish indeed now over the fantasies she'd wound around the invitation. More than foolish. She felt like a balloon which had just been pricked.

'What? You've met Bandar already? Why didn't you say so?'

'Because it was just so embarrassing. I didn't realise he was who he was at first, Cleo,' Samantha said dispiritedly. 'I thought he was just a groom. And a gypsy to boot.'

'A gypsy! Well, he does look a bit like a gypsy, I suppose. With that hair and skin and eyes. But, Samantha, for pity's sake, he doesn't look or act anything like a groom! So tell me. What on earth happened?'

Samantha told her the horrible truth, though she didn't add the genuinely humiliating part about how she'd thought he might have fancied her.

'Oh, Samantha,' Cleo exclaimed, half-laughing, half-chiding. 'One day you'll have to learn to put your brain into gear before you open your mouth. Men hate aggressive women. That's your main problem, you know, love. You're way too aggressive.'

'I prefer to think of myself as assertive,' Samantha defended, though a bit more lamely than usual.

'Same thing. But not to worry. It's not as though you're trying to come on to the Sheikh. I mean, men like that…' Her voice trailed off knowingly.

'I'm well aware of the kind of women men like that go for, Cleo,' Samantha said drily.

'Unfortunately not short, plump, fifty-year-old married women having a bad hair day,' Cleo quipped back.

Now it was Samantha's turn to laugh. Cleo always made her laugh. She was going to miss her when she left.

Cleo sighed in that wistful way women had been sighing since time began. 'My, but he *is* very attractive, isn't he?'

'I suppose so. If you like male chauvinist pigs.'

'Samantha, truly, he's no such thing! He's just as charming as Ali. In fact, Bandar's much more charming than Ali was when he first came here. Must be all those years he's lived in London, mixing with the upper crust.'

'I can see he's charmed you all right. I'll bet the men don't think he's quite so charming.'

'You might be wrong about that. He was lovely to Jack. I measure a man's character by how he treats Jack. And how Jack responds to him. Animals and children can't be fooled.'

Women could be, though, Samantha thought privately. Give a man looks and wealth, and women seemed to become blind to their faults and flaws.

Samantha had always thought she was above such nonsense. But it seemed she wasn't. She suspected that if the Sheikh wanted to charm her, he probably could. Look at the way she'd been constantly thinking about him since their brief encounter.

She had to stop it.

'Is there anything I can do to help?' she offered. 'Norm mentioned you were pretty busy. And Gerald isn't expecting me back on the job till tomorrow morning.'

'No, I'm on top of things now. And I have Judy coming in later, to help with the cooking and serving.'

'What are you going to cook?'

'No idea yet. Nothing too flash or complicated. Roast lamb, probably. With home-baked bread. And some of my quince pie and cream afterwards. Ali loves that menu, so it should be all right. I'm not sure about an entrée. I might just put out some nibbles to have with drinks beforehand.'

'He won't drink if he's a Muslim,' Samantha pointed out.

'Gosh, you're right. I didn't think of that. I'll ask him when he gets back what his attitude to alcohol is. Ali always serves it, though he doesn't drink it himself. But the men will be expecting a beer or two. Especially Ray. Trevor, too. And Gerald loves wine with a meal. Look, I'm sure he won't mind the others having a drink. He's a sophisticated man, and he's lived in London most of his life. He must be used to the western world's drinking habits by now.'

'If he isn't, he soon will be out here,' Samantha said drily. Australian men loved their beer.

'Did Bandar give you a time to be up here?' Cleo asked.

'He said eight.'

'Oh, dear—that late? By the time everyone has a drink and a chat it'll be nearly nine before you all sit down to eat. I sure hope he doesn't expect me to serve up dinner at that ungodly hour *every* night. I know people who live in Europe eat late in the evenings, but we don't. Not up here in the country, anyway. Still, he's the boss, I guess. I'll just have to put up with it till Ali gets back. But I'm going to miss all my favourite TV shows. Oh-oh—I hear someone on the gravel outside. I think he's back. Gotta go, love. See you tonight.'

Tonight, Samantha thought with a shudder as she clicked off her phone.

Already she was looking forward to it. And dreading it.

'I'm a bloody fool!' she growled, just as her mobile phone rang.

'Yes?' she said sharply.

'Sam. It's me—Gerald. A little birdie told me you were back. Look, I could do with a hand. One of the weanlings has slipped in some mud near a gate and gashed its front leg. A colt, of course. I need someone to keep him calm while I stitch him up. Do you think you could come? You seem to have a special touch with colts.'

Samantha was only too glad to do something. The thought of sitting around the cottage, getting herself into a state about tonight, did not appeal.

'I'll be right there,' she said.

'Great! See you soon, then.'

Samantha slipped back into her leather jacket, her spirits lifting immediately. Working with horses always made her feel good. Because she was good at it. No one could ever take that away from her.

To hell with men, she thought as she headed for the door. Give me horses any day!

CHAPTER THREE

DARK fell long before eight o'clock. The days were short at this time of the year, with the temperature dropping sharply once the sun sank behind the mountain range, especially on nights like this, which were clear of cloud. A full moon hung low in the sky, bathing the valley in its silvery light and making the huge white house on the hill stand out even more.

Samantha left the cottage right on eight, knowing full well it would take her another couple of minutes to drive back to the fork in the road, then up the hill to the house. She was determined not to be right on time, as ordered by the Sheikh. But not late enough to be seriously rude.

She was also determined not to surrender to temptation and try to doll herself up for this dinner. The others there tonight would think it odd. They were used to the way she looked and dressed. Cleo might roll her eyes at her choice of clothes, but that was too bad.

Her boot-leg blue jeans were clean. So were her elastic-sided riding boots. Her black roll-neck was as good as new and not too warm. The house was well insulated, and air-conditioned, though she suspected that the fire-places would be lit tonight. Samantha had put on her black leather jacket for the drive up, but would remove it once she was inside.

She'd decided against make-up, despite now owning quite a bit and being able to apply all of it reasonably well. Cleo had left no stone unturned before sending her off last week on her mission impossible.

Samantha reasoned she hadn't been wearing any make-up earlier today, when she'd met the Sheikh, so she wasn't about to plaster any on tonight. Not even lipstick. The same thing with perfume. She had, however, freshly shampooed, conditioned and dried her hair—for fear it might smell of horses—but she'd pulled it back and fastened it at the nape of her neck with a black clip. No way did she want him thinking she was trying to look sexy for him by wearing her hair down.

She took her time driving up the hill, noting the now empty helipad with a mixture of surprise and irritation. That she'd missed hearing the helicopter's departure was an indictment on her distracted state of mind. The darn thing was horribly noisy. Admittedly she'd put her stereo on fairly loudly when she'd arrived back at the cottage around five. Possibly the helicopter had left during the time she was inside. Hopefully, it had. She didn't like to think she was totally losing it.

The other three staff members coming to the dinner had arrived by the time she pulled up her vehicle in the guest parking area to the side of the house. Gerald's very dusty four-wheel drive was parked between Trevor's battered ute and Ray's equally worse-for-wear blue truck.

Country men, Samantha had quickly come to realise last year, weren't as car-mad as city guys. All they required from a vehicle was that it did the job required. Both Ray and Trevor were dyed-in-the-wool bachelors in their late forties, not at all interested in attracting women, so their vehicles were even worse than most.

Samantha was very attached to her forest-green four-wheel drive, bought not long before she left Sydney. She liked to keep it clean and polished and performing well.

Samantha guided it smoothly to a halt on the gravel beside Trevor's ute, leaving the keys in the ignition when she alighted. No one was going to steal it here.

She carried no bag with her. There would be no titivating tonight—unlike last week, when she'd run off to the nearest powder room all the time, to check her make-up and hair. She knew *exactly* what she looked like tonight.

Her tomboy image was reflected in Cleo's exasperated expression when she answered the front door.

'I know I said there wasn't any point in batting your eyelashes at our VIP visitor,' Cleo muttered as she closed the door behind Samantha. 'But truly, girl, a little practice wouldn't go astray. On top of that, you're late. I don't think Bandar is pleased. He was just asking me where you were.'

Samantha liked the thought of the Sheikh not being pleased. But she didn't show it. She just shrugged in feigned indifference as she removed her leather jacket and hung it in the coat closet which came off the spacious foyer. 'I'm only a few minutes late. I presume everyone's in the front room?' She was well acquainted with the layout of the house, having traipsed around after Cleo on several occasions.

'Yes—so get yourself in there, pronto. I have a roast to attend to.' And Cleo was off, a bustling bundle of energy, dressed tonight in an emerald-green velour tracksuit.

Cleo was as far removed from a cliché housekeeper as one could get. No dreary black dresses for her, or severely scraped-back hair. Cleo's hair was very short, very spiky, and very red. Her lipstick tonight was just as bright.

Once alone, Samantha glanced to her right at the shut double doors. Like all the doors in the house, they were very grand, made of a rich cedar, carved in a middle eastern style, with huge brass doorknobs. Behind these, she knew, was a formal reception room, with brocade-covered sofas and chairs arranged around an enormous marble fireplace. The fire would be lit tonight, making the expensive furniture glow and the chandelier above gleam as only a crystal chandelier could.

Steeling herself, Samantha reached for the right door knob, turned it, and pushed the door open.

'Ah—here's Sam now,' Gerald announced as she walked in.

Samantha had heard stories about people in stressful circumstances imagining that everything around them seemed suddenly frozen, like a tableau. Maybe that was going too far, but her step definitely faltered. Her eyes swiftly bypassed Gerald, who was sitting in an armchair, holding a glass of sherry, before flicking over Trevor and Ray, both of whom were perched uncomfortably at either end of the main sofa, glasses of beer in their hands, and finally landing on the man standing to one side of the softly glowing fire, his left elbow leaning on the marble mantelpiece, a crystal brandy balloon cupped in his right hand.

If Samantha had thought the Sheikh sexy earlier today, she now found him devastatingly so. He looked simply superb, in slimline black trousers and a royal blue silk shirt, the design of which was not dissimilar in style from that of the white shirt he'd had on earlier. Open-necked, its long sleeves were fuller than a business shirt, gathered in at the cuffs. He still didn't look like a sheikh, but no longer like a gypsy. His black wavy hair was too well groomed, his face freshly shaved, his appearance immaculate.

He did still look exotic. And not quite of this world. Samantha could see him playing the part of a buccaneer—a very wealthy one, by the look of his jewellery.

Several large rings graced his elegantly long fingers. One had a black centre stone, the second a diamond, the third a huge blue sapphire. Undoubtedly all were real. A thick gold watch encircled his left wrist. A thinner but probably even more expensive gold chain hung around his neck, the end nestling in the wispy curls of chest hair exposed by the deep V of the shirt.

His head had turned at her entry, his black eyes raking over her from top to toe. They did not flash at her this time, either with admiration or amusement. But there was something in their depths which compelled her to keep staring at him. She literally could not take her eyes away from his, could not move.

But there was movement inside her. A hot rushing of blood. A feeling not of being frozen, but of melting.

'I was beginning to worry something might have happened to you,' he said, an impatient edge in his voice.

Ray made a sniggering sound. 'Not likely. Sam's not that kind of girl—are you, Sam?'

'And what kind of girl *am* I, Ray?' Samantha whipped back, irritated by the remark, yet grateful for the distraction. At last she managed to look away from the Sheikh, close the door behind her and walk further into the room.

'Not the kind who gets herself into trouble,' Ray said with a dry laugh.

'Any woman can get herself into trouble,' the Sheikh remarked, his softly delivered words drawing Samantha's eyes once more.

'Come,' he commanded. 'I'll get you a drink.' And he gestured for her to follow him over to the long sideboard under the front windows, where Cleo always put the drinks and the glasses.

Samantha was startled that he would personally be getting her a drink. Cleo had said he didn't stand on ceremony, but Samantha hadn't found the owner of Smoking Gun of an easygoing or casual nature earlier today. He'd been downright arrogant and autocratic in his manner towards her.

Possibly he was a chameleon of a male, depending on his mood and the occasion. She'd met plenty of moody men in her time. Her father was moody. So were a couple of her brothers. Moody, and occasionally mean. One good thing about coming to live in the country had been finally moving out of home. When she returned to Sydney she would buy a place of her own. She had plenty of savings—enough for a deposit on a house.

'What can I get you?' he asked, slanting a questioning glance over at her as she joined him by the sideboard. 'Spirits? Wine? Or something softer?'

Was that a slight smirk she glimpsed in his eyes when he said the word *softer*?

'You don't have to serve me,' she returned stiffly. 'I am quite capable of getting myself a drink.'

Now he smiled. Definitely a smile of amusement.

'I am sure you are,' he said smoothly. 'But that is not the point. A gentleman always gets a lady her drink,' he added, and flashed her a warm smile.

Samantha gritted her teeth. He was determined to have his way, either by using his authority to order her around or by laying on the charm. Of course men like him were used to having their own way. Used to exercising their charm over women as well. Cleo had already fallen victim to it. Now *she* was in danger of following suit. The man was almost irresistible when he smiled like that.

And didn't he know it!

This last thought made Samantha resolve not to surrender to his charm. Different, perhaps, if he'd been an ordinary man. But swooning over a billionaire playboy sheikh not only went against her grain, it was a total waste of time. Much more so even than her getaway to the Gold Coast.

'A glass of white wine will do,' she said offhandedly, as though she didn't give a hoot what she drank, or who she drank with.

But as she watched him draw a bottle of Chardonnay out of the ice-bucket and pour the chilled wine into a glass, her treacherous body refused to obey her head. Standing this close to him was doing strange things to her.

Not only had her heart started racing, but all her senses seemed suddenly to be heightened. Never before had she been conscious of how a man smelled—perhaps because the men she was around mostly smelled of horses.

Bandar didn't smell of horses. Not in the slightest. The scent wafting from his body was as exotic as he was: something spicy, sensual and sexy. Oh, yes, very sexy.

'I am told this wine comes from an excellent local vineyard,' he said, as he held the glass out in her direction.

She turned to take it and their eyes met once more, his again flicking from her face to her feet, then back up again. Not with admiration this time, either. Curiosity, perhaps?

Samantha winced inside. She knew what he was thinking. What kind of woman was this, who cared nothing for her appearance?

Embarrassment besieged her, plus a perverse regret that she hadn't taken some trouble with her appearance tonight. Her tongue raced to her rescue, as it always did when she found herself feeling vulnerable in male company.

'I thought Muslims didn't drink,' she said sharply, when he picked up his brandy balloon again.

He took a sip before lowering the glass from his mouth. 'Some do,' he replied, eyeing her with curiosity. 'The world is full of imperfect people. But I am not Muslim.'

That took her aback. 'Oh. Sorry. I just presumed. Most of you are.'

His dark brows lifted. 'Most of *who* are?'

'Arabs.'

'Some Arabs are Christian,' he pointed out. 'Some

are Jewish. Some are even Buddhists and atheists. But I am not any of those, either.'

'Then what are you?' she threw at him.

'I am who I am.'

'Which is what?'

'Just a man named Bandar.'

'A *sheikh* named Bandar,' she corrected. Samantha hated false modesty. He was no ordinary man, this Bandar. He was a billionaire, for starters.

'Yes, I am a sheikh. But it is merely an inherited title. I prefer not to capitalise on it. Some people I mix with in London like to address me as Sheikh because it makes them feel important. I'm sure you are not one of those. So please…call me Bandar.'

'Suits me,' she said with a shrug. 'We call everyone by their first names here in Australia. Except perhaps the Prime Minister.'

'And what do you call him?'

'Depends on whether we're happy with his policies or not,' she quipped, feeling more comfortable with this kind of conversation. It was what she was used to being with men: slightly caustic, not in any way tongue-tied or vulnerable.

He stared at her, then shook his head. 'I think I have a lot to learn about Australians,' he said. 'It is a pity I will only be here for three weeks. I suspect it might take considerably longer to understand your very different culture.'

'A lot of people don't think Australians have *any* culture.'

He looked at her hard again. 'You are a most unusual woman. We will talk later. Over dinner. But for now there are a few things I must say to the others. Do sit down,' he ordered, before striding back towards the fireplace.

Samantha sat down. There was a time and place for outright rebellion and this was not it. Besides, she suddenly *needed* to sit down, her verbal sparring with Bandar having left her feeling oddly weak, as though she'd used up all her resistance to him.

Not that it really mattered.

Her capacity to resist this man was never going to be challenged. Or tested.

Nevertheless, her eyes followed him slavishly as he took his position at the mantelpiece once more.

'Thank you for coming to dine with me this evening,' he began, his manner now very formal and serious. 'Before we retire to the dining room for our meal I have a few things I wish to make clear. Firstly, I want to reassure you that Prince Ali has the fullest confidence in all his staff here, especially his stallion and mare managers,' he said, dipping his head slightly towards Ray and Trevor. 'He has not put me in charge to interfere with the general running of this establishment, but to be here to make decisions if decisions need to be made. Fortunately, it is not a busy time. Foaling in your country does not begin till August. But thoroughbreds are sensitive creatures, notorious for causing unexpected problems. If a problem arises, please refer it to me. I am a very experienced racehorse owner and breeder. There is nothing I do not know about this industry.'

Samantha tried not to look askance at this rather egotistical statement. She already knew that Bandar was arrogant. But, truly, was there anyone on the world who knew *everything* about horses?

'Having touched on the subject of my horsemanship,' he continued. 'I know there was considerable dissention amongst you about my riding Smoking Gun on the track today. You, Raymond, expressed some reservations at the time. Gerald also. And Samantha—who happened to pass by the track at that particular time—was quite disturbed. She thought what I was doing was reckless and risky. And said so in no uncertain terms.'

Samantha straightened in her chair when her three colleagues swung round to give her looks which proclaimed that she obviously didn't know which side her bread was buttered on. Naturally, she hadn't mentioned her run-in with Bandar when she'd been working with them this afternoon. But now that it was out in the open she wasn't about to back down.

'I still think exactly the same thing,' she said without hesitation. After all, what could he do to her? Have her fired? She was quitting soon, anyway.

'Why am I not surprised?' the Sheikh muttered, his dark eyes glittering at her. 'But you are wrong, madam. I know that horse inside out, and I know what he needs to make him behave himself. He has behaved since then, has he not?' he directed at the stallion manager.

'Been like a lamb,' Ray concurred.

'He will, however, not be so lamb-like in a few more days—at which point I will ride him again. I trust there will be no further objections. Now, do any of you have any questions?' he asked, his gaze settling back on Samantha.

She held his steady regard without visible squirming, which was a minor miracle. She was certainly squirming inside.

'Ali was gunna go to a dispersal sale this Wednesday,' Trevor piped up in his broad Aussie accent. 'The owner of one of the local stud farms around here died six months ago. His wife is sellin' up everything and movin' back to the city. The mares are real quality. Some of 'em are in foal to top-line stallions. I know Ali was real keen to attend.'

'I see. I shall ring Ali tomorrow and talk to him about it. If he is agreeable, I will go to this sale in his stead. But I might need a driver for the day.'

'Sam could drive you,' Gerald suggested. 'She could check over any mares you might like the look of at the same time. Sam doesn't miss a trick, and she's got a good eye for a horse.'

Samantha's stomach flipped over when Bandar looked at her. 'Is that agreeable with you, Samantha?'

Goodness, what a question! It was *not* agreeable. It was breathtakingly exciting and extremely worrying. How could she function properly with him by her side for a whole day?

Somehow she gave a nonchalant shrug of her shoulders. 'You're the boss,' she said, as though the matter was of no consequence to her.

He smiled a small, enigmatic smile. 'I will let you know before tomorrow evening if I will require you on Wednesday. Now I think it is time for us to retire to the dining room.'

CHAPTER FOUR

THE table in the formal dining room was huge, capable of seating at least twenty people. Cleo had set only one end: her VIP visitor clearly expected to grace the head of the table, with two settings on either side of him. A huge bowl of fresh flowers sat in the middle of the long table, which meant it would be totally useless for hiding behind.

Samantha swiftly slipped into one of the chairs furthest from the end, grateful when Gerald sat down next to her, with Ray and Trevor taking up the two settings opposite. Bandar made himself comfortable at the head of the table, shooting her a sharp glance as he flicked out his serviette.

Ignoring him, she shook out her own serviette with slow, considered movements and placed it on her lap, her eyes fixed on the connecting door through which she hoped Cleo would soon come.

She did, carrying a tray laden with steaming bowls of soup.

'You decided to serve an entrée after all?' Samantha whispered, when Cleo placed her bowl in front of her.

'You should have known that by the arrangement of cutlery,' Cleo whispered back.

Samantha didn't like to tell her that the arrangement of cutlery had been the last thing she'd been thinking about when she'd sat down at this table.

'I hope the menu will be to your liking, Bandar,' Cleo said, when she returned to the dining room with a plateful of herb bread. 'It's one of Ali's favourite meals. Sweet potato and leek soup, followed by roast minted lamb, finished off with quince pie. Home-made too, of course. We have a lovely quince tree on the farm,' she added, pride in her voice.

'I can see why Ali never wants to travel,' the Sheikh replied. 'He is looked after too well here.'

'Oh, go on with you,' Cleo said, and actually gave him a playful nudge on his upper arm.

He looked momentarily shocked. Then amused.

'Oh, dear—I've forgotten the wine!' Cleo suddenly exclaimed. 'I'll go get it right now.'

'Make mine red,' Gerald called out to Cleo as she hurried back towards the door which led into the kitchen.

'I have both opened,' she returned over her shoulder. 'Never fear.'

'Ali told me his housekeeper was a treasure,' Bandar said warmly whilst Cleo was out of the room. 'I can see what he means. She is like a breath of fresh air. Under other circumstances, I might try to steal her away.'

'You wouldn't stand a chance of doing that under *any* circumstances,' Samantha jumped in, before she could think better of it. 'Cleo would never leave Ali, or his family. *Or* Australia.'

His dark eyes glittered at her like they had once before, when she'd challenged him over Smoking Gun.

'You would be amazed how such things become irrelevant with the right offer of money,' he said, that edge back in his voice.

Just then Cleo re-entered the room, carrying a bottle of white wine in an ice-bucket, plus a decanter filled with red wine. She placed them both on the table within easy reach of everyone.

'If I paid you a million dollars a year, Cleo,' Bandar said silkily, 'would you come with me back to London?'

'That depends as what,' she shot back with a cheeky smile.

'My personal chef.'

Cleo pulled a face. 'Sorry. Now, if you'd said mistress, I might have considered it.'

Everyone laughed, even Samantha. But not for long. Soon she was just sitting there, staring down blankly at the soup and wishing she could be more like Cleo. That woman was never rattled by anything. She was so good with people, and had the most delightful sense of humour. It was a shame that she and Norm had never had children. She'd have made a wonderful mother.

This last thought gave rise to her own aspirations about one day being a mum. Hopefully, that was possible. Samantha had known for some years that she might have some trouble conceiving. She was shockingly irregular when she wasn't on the Pill.

Even if she *did* have a baby one day, would she be a good mother? What if she had a girl? A girl needed a mother who was feminine, who could show her how to act like a girl. How could she do that when she couldn't do it herself?

Adult life, Samantha had discovered, was full of

many unexpected complications and pitfalls. Being a child was much simpler—though perhaps not so simple when you didn't have a mother yourself.

'Didn't you like my soup?'

Cleo's aggrieved question brought Samantha back to the real world, where she discovered that everyone had finished their soup but she was still sitting there, with hers hardly touched.

'Oh, sorry, Cleo. Yes, it's lovely,' she said, taking a hurried mouthful. 'I was daydreaming. Leave it with me. I'll finish it. I promise.'

'Nope,' Cleo said, whipping the bowl away. 'You've lost your chance. Judy has the next course ready to serve.'

Which she did, placing a dinner plate in front of Samantha before she could say boo. It looked and smelled delicious, but somewhere along the line Samantha had lost her appetite. She sighed as she picked up her knife and fork, knowing she would have to force some down or Cleo would be totally disgusted with her.

This dinner party was proving to be an even worse trial than she'd imagined it would be. And what of Wednesday? How would she cope if Bandar wanted her to go to that dispersal sale with him? She'd have to spend the whole day with him. Alone.

Samantha had been unhappy with herself for a long time. Around the Sheikh, however, she was close to despising herself. If Cleo had been twenty-six, single and in her position, she wouldn't have come here tonight dressed in jeans with her hair all scraped back from her un-made-up face. Cleo would have been done up to the nines. She'd have flattered the Sheikh, flirted with him, and had a great time. He'd have been totally charmed, and probably would have ended up taking her back to London with him. Or at least taking her to bed.

He'd be good in bed. No, Samantha amended ruefully in her mind. He'd be *very* good.

Not that you'll ever find out, girl.

But she supposed she could *think* about it. And think about him.

Her eyes drifted sidewards and up to where Bandar was sitting, at the head of table, chatting away with Gerald, who was doing most of the talking—asking the Sheikh about his racehorses in England. It seemed Bandar owned an obscene number of champions, which showed just how rich he was. He had started eating his lamb, his eyes dropping to his plate, though his head remained tipped slightly in Gerald's direction.

Her surreptitious gaze fastened on his mouth, her own mouth drying as she watched his lips open and close over the food. He was a slow, sensual eater, licking his lips occasionally, his facial expression when he swallowed one of immense satisfaction.

Samantha could have watched him eat all night.

'Did you buy Smoking Gun as a yearling?' Ray suddenly piped up.

When Bandar glanced up and caught her staring at him Samantha could have died on the spot. His eyes narrowed on her for a split second before he put down his knife and fork and looked over at Ray, leaving her feeling humiliated once more.

'No, I bred him. I breed most of my horses. That gives me a lot of satisfaction.'

'You must've started breeding pretty young,' Gerald

remarked. 'Smoking Gun is six, and you can't be more than thirty.'

'Thank you for the compliment, but I will turn thirty-five this year.'

Samantha wasn't surprised that he was older than he looked. His face *was* unlined, unlike the other weatherbeaten men at the table, but there was a wealth of experience in his eyes.

'I inherited my father's stud farm when I was only sixteen. So, yes, I started young.'

Samantha imagined he would have started *everything* young.

'Has he always been such a handful?' Ray asked. 'Smoking Gun I'm talking about.'

'Not at all. He was extremely tractable during his racing career. But his new life at stud has excited him somewhat. Still, we men can surely understand that. There is nothing more stimulating than that time in a young male's life when he first discovers the pleasures of the flesh. And Smoking Gun has suddenly gone from servicing several mares a day to total celibacy. A frustrating situation for any virile male animal,' he said, his dark eyes sliding back down the table to Samantha.

His gaze was not in any way provocative, yet she found her breath catching in her throat and her mind conjuring up hidden messages both in his words and his eyes. She started imagining he was talking about himself, not his horse. That he was telling her his sex life had suddenly gone from a feast to a famine and he wasn't any happier about it than his stallion.

'Come springtime he will be as good as gold,' he went on, releasing her gaze as he flashed a warm smile around the table. 'From what Ali has told me, he has a veritable harem of the finest broodmares awaiting him here.'

'He sure has,' Trevor confirmed. 'His book is chock-a-block.'

'Lucky horse,' Bandar murmured, those dark eyes slanting briefly Samantha's way before dropping back to his food.

Samantha reached for her glass of wine and took a big gulp, telling herself she was suffering from a seriously over-active imagination. There were no hidden messages in his eyes. He wasn't interested in her. He *couldn't* be. She was a fool.

And from that moment nothing the Sheikh said or did could have been even remotely misinterpreted as a come-on. In fact he ignored her, with any conversation directed entirely at the men.

Not that he made much conversation from that point on. To be honest, by the time dessert arrived he'd begun to look tired. His dark eyes had developed even darker hollows around them. A few times he rubbed at his temple, frowning in that way people did when they weren't feeling all that well, or when something was on their mind.

After he'd eaten less than half of Cleo's large serving of quince pie, he abruptly put his fork down and stood up.

'I must apologise,' he said, his voice as strained as his face. 'It seems that jet lag has suddenly caught up with me and I must retire. I'll speak to Cleo on my way out. Reassure her it was not her cooking. I bid you good night. I will see you all in the morning. *Insh'allah*,' he added, with a somewhat wry twist to his mouth.

And he was gone.

'Well!' Gerald exclaimed. 'That was a bit rude. It wouldn't have hurt him to last till coffee.'

'He didn't look well,' Samantha said defensively, annoyed with Gerald for being so unsympathetic. Couldn't he see the man was all done in? Jet lag was known to strike quickly. Not that she'd ever experienced any. She hadn't been out of Australia. Another matter she would address in the near future. They said travel broadened the mind. Hers could certainly do with some broadening. She'd actually got herself a passport last year, after she'd left her job with Paul, but wasn't quite sure what she was going to do.

'What was that Arab thing he said?' Trevor asked. '*Insha* somethin' or other?'

'Got no idea,' Gerald replied. 'Never heard Ali say it.'

'Ask him,' Trevor said to Gerald.

'*You* ask him,' Gerald shot back.

'Oh, for pity's sake—what does it matter?' Samantha said irritably. 'He'll be gone by the end of June. He's only staying three weeks.'

'Thank God,' Ray muttered. 'He's not a patch on Ali.'

Samantha almost opened her mouth to defend him again, but shut it just in time. She didn't want them thinking she fancied him.

Bad enough that she did.

Wednesday popped back into her mind as she drove back to the cottage a short time later. Did she still not want to go with him?

The answer came to her as she lay in her lonely bed that night and wound the most impossible fantasies about the man.

Despite fearing she might make a fool of herself if she was alone with him, Samantha *did* want to go—if only to keep feeling the things he could make her feel. And think the things he could make her think. Exciting things. Sexual things…

In her head, they were riding together—Bandar on a big grey stallion, she on a lovely chestnut mare with a white blaze on her chest. They stopped on a riverbank where he lifted her off her horse, holding her close whilst his eyes travelled all over her flushed face. He kissed her hungrily. Not once, but several times. She was breathless by the time his head lifted from her mouth. He reached for the buttons on her shirt and undid them, one at a time. She was naked underneath. He spoke no words as he stripped her to the waist. He just stared at her. Her nipples tightened under his gaze. She wanted him to touch her breasts but he didn't. He laid her down on the soft grass and removed the rest of her clothes. The day was sunny, but not warm. Yet she wasn't cold. Her shivers were those of desire. She called out his name and he told her not to speak. She stared up at him as he took his own clothes off. His body was beautiful. He lay down next to her on the grass and began to stroke her. She couldn't bear it. She wanted him inside her. She told him, and he smiled. He kept touching her…teasing her. She sobbed her frustration. She told him that she loved him…

'What a load of bunkum!' Samantha muttered as she sat up abruptly and gave her pillow a frustrated punch.

Okay, so Bandar was attractive and sexy and sophisticated and rich, and just about everything a fantasy lover should be.

But the feelings he evoked in her had nothing to do with love. Samantha might be personally inexperienced, but she was an intelligent girl, living in the twenty-first century. Just because she hadn't felt this level of sexual attraction before, it didn't mean she couldn't recognise it when it hit.

Lust was what was making her head spin and her heart race when she was around the Sheikh. Not love.

Samantha lay back down, satisfied that she'd got that straight.

But knowing what was ailing her didn't make it any easier to bear. Letting her head fill with silly fantasies wasn't helping, either. It just left her feeling restless and wretched.

The sooner that infernal man went back to London, the better. And the sooner *she* went back to Sydney, the better. She needed to get on with her life. Real life. Not this foolish fantasy she'd been indulging in tonight.

Till that happened, some pragmatism was called for. Plus some common sense and composure. There was no need to get all in a knot if she had to go with Bandar on Wednesday. All she had to do was do her job and keep her silly infatuated self in check.

Surely she could do that?

Meanwhile, tonight there would no more weaving of imaginary sexual scenarios involving herself and the Sheikh.

Samantha snapped on her bedside lamp and picked up the novel she usually read at bedtime. It was an involving and complicated thriller, full of assassins and government agents and impossible plot surprises. Best of all, there was not even a hint of romance in it.

Perfect.

She sat up, propped a couple of pillows behind her, and started to read.

CHAPTER FIVE

JUNE in eastern Australia was the first month of winter. At this time of year in the upper Hunter Valley the temperature at night often fell below zero, with a frost by the morning. But then the sun would come out and the temperature would rise, often to a very pleasant twenty degrees.

Wednesday promised to be just such a day.

Samantha woke early, when the frost was still on the ground and the sun not yet risen, and the immediate curling of her stomach reminded her that, yes, it was Wednesday. And, yes, she was going to spend the day with Bandar at the dispersal sale.

His absence around the stud the day before had provided her with some respite from his disturbing presence. But the moment he'd called her late yesterday afternoon, informing her that he *would* be going to the dispersal sale and she was to pick him up at the house at nine the next morning, all her pragmatic resolve had vanished and her world had tipped off its axis again.

She'd found it difficult to get to sleep. She'd read her

bedside book into the small hours of the morning and actually finished the darned thing before sheer exhaustion had done the trick. But here she was, awake again, and it was only five-thirty. Three and a half hours to go before she was due to pick Bandar up.

Samantha had a feeling they were going to be the longest three and a half hours of her life.

She was right. Not only were they the longest, but the most trying. Common sense demanded that she not make any drastic changes to her appearance. But what was common sense in the face of female vanity?

In the end, she simply *had* to make some changes. But not to her clothes. She just teamed her oldest and most comfortable blue jeans with a long-sleeved blue and red checked shirt which didn't show the dirt.

Her face, however, she gave considerable thought to. She wanted to look as natural as possible. But she still wanted to look as good as she could.

Instead of foundation—which might be obvious in the daylight—she smoothed on a tinted sunscreen-moisturiser, which the cosmetic salesgirl had claimed would soften and even out her skin tones, and stop her getting freckles at the same time.

Samantha was happy with the result.

Next came her eyes. She decided against eyeshadow for the same reason she'd discarded the idea of foundation. Too obvious in daylight. Mascara, however, would not be. So she applied a couple of coats till her normally fine eyelashes were thick and dark, bringing out the blue in her eyes.

Lipstick caused her a dilemma. She'd bought really bright ones for her getaway—deep pink, red and burgundy. What she needed was something closer to the colour of her lips. In the end, she rubbed a little Vaseline over them. Less was more. Or so they said.

She waffled for a while over perfume. Should she or shouldn't she spray on some of the designer-brand scent she'd also bought for her getaway?

'Maybe just a little,' Samantha told herself as she picked up the bottle and aimed some behind her ears.

Last came the decision about her hair. She'd already blowdried it straight, the cleverly cut layers making it surprisingly easy to style, and Samantha had to admit that it looked great down and around her face. More than great—it looked sexy.

That last thought did it. Up her hair went into a ponytail. It was one thing to look good today, quite another to try and be sexy. That was the way to further foolishness and humiliation.

The old wall clock in the kitchen finally pronounced it was time to leave. With butterflies already gathering in her stomach, Samantha picked up her trusty blue denim jacket—in case the weather turned nasty—and headed for the door. At five to nine she was pulling into the guest parking area beside the house on the hill.

Cleo didn't answer the front door, as Samantha expected. Instead Bandar stood there, carrying a picnic basket.

He didn't look tired any more. He looked refreshed and absolutely fabulous, in black jeans and a white polo-necked top. No rings graced his fingers, she noted, but he was wearing a stunning silver watch. His black wavy hair was faintly damp, giving rise to an image which Samantha tried to immediately banish, but couldn't.

Thinking of him naked, in the shower, was not conducive to calming the butterflies still crowding her stomach.

'Cleo said there will not be any food provided at the sale,' he explained, when Samantha stared down at the picnic basket. 'She packed us some lunch. She said our destination is a picturesque property, with lots of nice spots for a picnic.'

A feeling of panic joined Samantha's nerves. But she kept her expression poker-faced. 'Fine,' she said. 'Shall we go?'

'I am all yours,' he returned.

All hers. Now, wasn't that a laugh? He hadn't even looked at her properly. Just a cursory glance. All that fuss and bother for nothing!

Samantha whirled and strode back down the steps, marching across the gravel to the four-by-four, her temper barely in check. Not that she was angry with him. Mostly it was with herself.

'Better put that basket in the back,' she advised sharply as she climbed in behind the wheel and started the engine. 'Looks like Cleo has packed enough for an army.'

He did so, just making it into the passenger seat before she began reversing.

'Are we in a hurry?' he remarked drily as he clicked in his seat belt. 'The auction does not start till one this afternoon.'

'Trevor gave me a catalogue. He's marked the mares he thinks are worth buying. There's ten. A full inspection of ten mares will take me all morning.'

'*I* will decide which mares you will inspect,' Bandar said, with a return to that haughty manner he'd adopted at their first meeting. 'And which ones I will bid on.'

Samantha gritted her teeth. But inside she was grateful. When he acted like that she didn't find him at all attractive. All she wanted to do was smack him one, right in his super-white teeth.

Keep it up, buster.

'How far to this stud farm?' he asked when they reached the highway and Samantha steered her wheel to the left, heading towards Scone.

'About thirty minutes.'

'Have you been there before?'

'Nope.'

'But you do know the way?'

'Ray gave me directions.'

'Some women are not good with directions.'

'As opposed to most men?' she shot back, slanting him a savage glance.

The shock on his face swiftly gave way to a rueful laugh.

'Like I said the first time we met, you are a very impertinent woman. But I like you all the same,' he added.

'Am I supposed to be grateful for that?'

She could feel his eyes on her, but kept her own eyes fixed on the road ahead this time.

'I did not realise you disliked me so much.'

Samantha winced. Did she really want to go down this path again? She had resolved to get past this kind of stroppy and self-destructive behaviour. Okay, so Bandar was a fair way up himself. But she supposed most men would be if they'd been born a sheikh with pots of money and people grovelling to them all the time.

'I don't dislike you,' she said. 'I just…resent your attitude.'

'What attitude is that?'

'In my country, it's rude to ride roughshod over other people's opinions.'

'Ride roughshod?' he repeated thoughtfully. 'That is a good expression. I like it. But surely I have not done that. I have just asserted my authority. Ali asked me to represent him at this sale. I must do what *I* think is best.'

'Ali chose his staff for their expertise. He listens to them. With respect, Trevor knows more about Australian broodmares than you do. He'd be seriously put out if you totally ignored his advice.'

'I see. Yes, I see. In that case, I will look at what your mare manager has marked in the catalogue. But I will not bid on them if I do not personally like them.'

'Or if *I* find some physical defect in them,' Samantha added, somewhat mischievously.

'I would not dream of bidding on a mare that you do not pass as one hundred per cent perfect.'

'Then you won't be bidding on much. There aren't too many perfect broodmares around. You might have to settle for pretty good.'

'I will settle for whatever you recommend, Samantha. Is that fair?'

'More than fair. Okay—now, why don't you have a look at the catalogue on the way there? It's in the glove box. You can study what's listed and see if there's anything which interests you. Do you have an age that you prefer in a broodmare?'

'Young,' he said, opening the glove box and drawing out the catalogue. 'I like them young. And I like them to have performed on the track. That ensures they have the right temperament to pass on. A lot of unraced mares are timid, as well as unsound.'

'I agree with you. Nervous Nellies don't make the best mothers.'

'Nervous Nellies? I have never heard that saying before. You have a lot of interesting expressions in Australia.'

'You have no idea. Most don't bear repeating. I'm sure that you have some interesting sayings as well. In fact, you said something the other night which made us all curious. *Insha* something-or-other?'

'*Insh'allah.*'

'Yes, that's it. What does it mean?'

'It means Allah willing. God willing.'

'That sounds religious. You said you weren't religious?'

'I do not like man-made religions. But I believe in Allah. And in an after-life. If you don't, everything is so pointless. Living. Dying. Especially dying.'

'I know what you mean,' Samantha said. 'My mother died shortly after I was born. It would be sad to think she isn't somewhere, looking over me.' Her heart lurched as it did whenever she thought of the mother she'd never known who had died so very young. 'But let's not talk of death. It's a depressing subject. We have a lovely day ahead of us, doing what we both like doing best.

'Looking at horses,' she added, when he shot her a quizzical glance.

He smiled. 'Already you know me well.'

'I know horsemen. I'm sure they're all the same the whole world over, whether they are rich or poor.'

'Undoubtedly. To a horseman, horses are everything. I could not live without them.'

'With your money, you'd never have to.'

'True,' he said. 'The trick is to stay alive.'

'I can't see you dying any time soon. Unless you break your silly neck riding Smoking Gun.'

When he looked at her and laughed Samantha finally started to relax, the tightness in her stomach uncurling, her grip on the steering wheel lessening. Her view of the day ahead gradually changed from panic to one of pleasurable anticipation. It would be challenging, seeing if she could find the true gems amongst all the fool's gold offered today. Interesting to see, too, if Bandar was as knowledgeable about horses as he claimed to be.

At the same time she would try hard not to think of him as a devastatingly sexy man, but as just another horse-lover.

A very wealthy horse-lover, admittedly. But there were plenty of those around. She'd mixed with many multimillionaire racehorse owners back in Sydney. She'd never been attracted to any as she was attracted to Bandar, but she'd envied quite a few.

'You are so lucky, Bandar, to be able to afford to buy any horse you want. I hope you know that.'

He glanced up from where he'd been studying the catalogue. 'I have never really thought about it. A man is either born rich or poor. After that it is up to him to make of his life what he will. Since my father died I have increased my wealth considerably through my own endeavours. I feel I have earned the right to buy whatever I want.'

Samantha did not argue with him, but she considered it was surely an advantage to be born rich.

'One day,' she said, 'I'm going to go to a top yearling sale and buy myself a simply fabulous colt.'

'Not a filly?'

'Oh, no. I much prefer colts.' She always had—right from the time she'd first become interested in horses.

'Top colts command high prices,' Bandar warned her.

'I earn good money. And one day I'll have my own veterinary practice and earn a whole lot more.'

'You have ambition.'

'Girls are allowed to have ambition in this country,' she pointed out, somewhat tartly.

'Might I remind you that I live in England?'

'Maybe, but you are still an Arab sheikh, born into a vastly different culture. Not so long ago you'd have had a harem full of female love-slaves. And you wouldn't have thought it wrong.'

'You are so right. Having a harem of female love-slaves is a most attractive prospect. A man is not by nature monogamous. Muslims are still allowed up to four wives.'

'But you are not Muslim.'

'Not Muslim, and not married.'

'You have a girlfriend back home in England?'

'I have three lady-friends.'

'*Three!* And they're happy with that arrangement?'

'They have not complained.'

Samantha supposed he hadn't got his playboy reputation for nothing. But, brother, three girlfriends at once was going beyond the pale. It was positively disgusting!

'And what about you, Samantha? You have a boy-friend?'

'Not at the moment,' she bit out, her temper on the rise again.

'You do not like men much, I fear.'

'I like men fine.'

'But you like horses more.'

'That's the pot calling the kettle black. You like horses much more than women. If you liked women, you wouldn't be treating them so badly. Now, I think we should drop this subject before I get really mad with you. We have to spend the day together, so let's just stick to the subject of horses in future. Agreed?'

When she glanced over at him he looked totally non-plussed, as though he did not know what to make of her.

'Okay, so I'm not a run-of-the-mill female,' she raced on, before the situation got out of hand. 'I'm opinionated and downright difficult at times. But I'm also straightforward and honest, which I hope makes up for a lot of personality flaws. And I do like you, Bandar, despite your questionable morals. Any man who loves horses as much as you do has to have some good points, though I'm not sure yet what they are.'

By now he was fairly gaping at her.

'I promise to be on my best behaviour for the rest of the day if you promise not to tell me any more about your unsavoury lifestyle back home. Deal?'

He just shook his head at her, his expression one of total exasperation. 'You are impossible!'

'Yes, but I'm also driving. Deal?'

'I do not have an *unsavoury lifestyle* back home,' he argued.

'You are sleeping with three different women at the same time. Is that not true?'

'No. It is *not* true,' he said indignantly. 'I go to each of their beds on different nights. I do not have them in the same bed at the same time.'

'Oh, terrific. Glad we got that straight. That makes *all* the difference.'

He sighed with what sounded like satisfaction. 'I am glad we got that straight as well. I do not wish you to think I am some kind of roué.'

Samantha gave up at that point. The man *was* a roué—with the morals of an alley cat! He *had* been alluding to his own sex life the other night, when he'd been talking about going from a feast to a famine.

Who knew how he was coping out here, with no one to warm his bed at night? Unless he'd already seconded some of the girl grooms! She wouldn't put it past him. The man was sex on legs. He'd only have to crook his finger at any of them and they'd come running. Some of them weren't half bad looking, either.

This train of thought was not at all comforting.

Thank goodness the turn-off that led to Valleyview Farm had come. Some horsey distraction was called for. Anything to push out of her mind the image of Bandar going from one woman's bed to another's, and then to yet another's…

The road they'd turned onto was a dirt road, full of ruts and bumps.

'How can this stud farm be one of any quality?' Bandar soon complained. 'They cannot even afford to seal their roads.'

Samantha had to laugh. 'This isn't *their* road. This is a *public* road. Welcome to Australia!'

CHAPTER SIX

CLEO had been right about Valleyview Farm. It was a very picturesque place, with lovely lawns and gardens surrounding the main homestead, providing any number of spots for them to eat their picnic lunch.

And what a lovely lunch Cleo had provided: cold chicken, salad, freshly baked breadsticks and the most delicious carrot cake, along with two small bottles of chilled white wine which Samantha found nestled in the bottom of the cooler.

After three solid hours of inspecting all the mares marked in the catalogue, both Samantha and Bandar were more than ready to eat. They made short work of the food, enjoying it under a not-too-shady tree, with the dappled sunshine providing some very pleasant warmth.

Samantha tucked in whilst sitting cross-legged on one corner of the picnic blanket Cleo had also packed. Bandar sat with his back up against the trunk of the tree, his long legs stretched out before him.

'That was great,' Samantha said after she'd finished her cake, proud of herself for not staring at Bandar too much while he ate this time. 'I was so hungry I could have eaten a horse.'

'It is as well that Cleo packed us a substantial lunch, then,' Bandar replied, smiling at her over the rim of his glass. He still had an inch or two of wine left. 'Eating a horse around here could be a very expensive meal. Especially the ones *you* picked out for me this morning.'

'Oh, I don't know. We could be lucky and get some of them quite cheaply.'

'No,' he said, and swallowed the rest of his wine. 'I do not think so.'

'I appreciate they're all well-bred mares, some with very good performances on the track, but seriously, Bandar,' she said, her voice dropping to a conspiratorial whisper so that a group of people nearby didn't hear her, 'the turn-out today hasn't been wonderful. I suppose more buyers might still show up during the afternoon. But there were surprisingly few people here this morning inspecting the horses. There are going to be some bargains at this auction. Trust me.'

'We will not be here for the auction this afternoon,' he announced unexpectedly, putting his glass back on the blanket before getting to his feet.

Samantha scrambled to her feet also, confused by this unexpected turn of events. 'What do you mean? Why won't we be here for the auction?'

He took his time, brushing some grass from his black jeans before answering her. 'I have already bought the five mares we selected. I paid for them when you went back to the car to get the picnic basket.'

'Paid for them?' she repeated, totally thrown by this development. 'How much did you pay for them?'

'Two million dollars.'

'Two *million!*' she squawked, so loudly that the group of people turned to stare at them. But she didn't care. 'Two million—for five mares worth not more than a hundred thousand each! If that,' Samantha added, her hands finding her hips in total exasperation. The man had more money than sense!

He eyed her up and down with some exasperation of his own. 'Valleyview Farm has agreed to organise transport to Ali's stud farm as part of the deal,' he said coolly.

'No kidding? They'd probably have agreed to send the lot to Dubar for the price you paid!'

'Hush,' he commanded, his eyes flashing annoyance. 'This is not the time or the place for you to argue with me. Pack up the basket. We can discuss this back in the car.'

Samantha felt like informing Bandar that she was Prince Ali's vet, not *his* personal lackey. But he was already striding across the lawns towards the parking area and her vehicle. She had no option but to do what he ordered, or leave everything behind.

Samantha could just hear what Cleo would say to her if she did that.

So she fairly threw everything into the basket, cracking one of the wine glasses in the process. Stuffing the blanket on top, she snatched the basket up by the handles and stomped after Bandar. He was waiting for her by the passenger door, his face as thunderous as her own. They did not say a word to each other till they were both in their seats, Samantha being the first to speak.

'The reason you come to a dispersal sale,' she snapped, 'is to get a bargain! You do not pay upfront—

especially well above the market price. If you'd asked me, I could have told you what those mares were worth. I didn't realise you had no idea. I thought you knew *everything* about horses!'

He'd certainly shown a lot of expertise when he'd inspected the mares alongside her. She'd been fascinated at how calmly the horses had stood for him as he'd run his hands over them. He'd talked to them at the same time, in soft murmurings, telling them how lovely they were.

She suspected, by the furious look on his face, that she was not about to be subjected to any soft murmurings.

'My dear Samantha,' he ground out, with his jaw clenched so hard the veins were standing out in his neck. 'A bargain is only a bargain if you are in need of one. I can afford to pay more, and I did.'

'But you weren't using your own money,' she countered. 'You were buying those mares for Ali.'

'Do you think I would use Ali's money in making such a deal? I paid for them personally. They are to be gifts to my good friend.'

Samantha grimaced. 'Oh. I...I didn't know that. Sorry.'

'And so you should be,' he reprimanded. 'You are one of those women who speaks first and thinks later. I always have a good reason for what I do. For your enlightenment, Ali mentioned to me yesterday that the owner of Valleyview Farm is an elderly lady in severe financial difficulties. Her now deceased husband was not a good businessman. Two million is nothing to me, but could mean everything to a poor widow at this time in her life.'

'Oh.' Once again Samantha was taken aback, and also ashamed—both by her outburst and her rash judgement of him. 'Sorry,' she mumbled, before lifting her chin and shooting him an exasperated look. 'But you might have said that was your intention in the first place!'

'It was not my original intention. It was a spur-of-the-moment decision. I was going to stay and bid a more than fair price for those mares at the auction, but I changed my mind. If you insist on total honesty—and it seems you value honesty a lot—it was you who made me decide not to stay and attend the auction.'

'Me? What has your not staying for the auction got to do with me?'

'I think you know,' he said, his eyes locking with hers and holding them.

Samantha's heart began to race behind her ribs. 'I have no idea what you're talking about,' she claimed.

His eyes narrowed on her. 'I do not believe you. You are a highly intelligent girl. Does it embarrass you to admit the attraction between us?'

'*What?*' Her eyes flared wide with shock, her mouth dropping open.

'Do not deny it. The chemistry has been there from the first moment we met. Though you did make me doubt it when you showed up for dinner that evening looking like you were about to muck out some stables. What kind of woman is this, I thought to myself, who does not try to enhance her natural beauty?'

'Huh!' came her automatic reaction. 'I have no natural beauty to enhance.'

His hand cupped her chin firmly and brought her face closer to his.

'You think your eyes are not beautiful?' he asked, his own truly beautiful eyes caressing hers in a way which would make any woman melt.

Samantha melted, then overheated as outrage joined in.

She smacked his hand away, her cheeks going bright red whilst her heart did a tango within her chest. 'Don't you dare flatter me just to get me into bed! I know what's ailing you, Mr Moneybags. You've had to leave your playboy lifestyle behind and you're missing it like mad. You've been almost a week without one of your three girlfriends, and you're feeling like a bit on the side. Well, I'm not going to be that bit. For *your* enlightenment,' she threw back at him, using the same expression he'd used earlier, 'I'm not in the business of being used by men—especially arrogant, up-themselves sheikhs with more money than morals.'

Her tirade seemed to shake him almost as much as it shook her. Samantha could not believe she was doing what she was doing. Her fantasy man wanted to take her to bed and she was knocking him back! Not only knocking him back but insulting him so much that he was sure never to ask her again. How self-destructive could you get?

Samantha was trembling all through her body as she pushed open the driver's door and leapt out of the four-wheel drive. Knowing that she'd ruined everything once more only made her madder.

'I am going to the ladies',' she spat out. 'When I come back, I am going to drive us back home. When we get there, you can explain to the men why we didn't stay for the auction. I'm sure Trevor will be thrilled that you bought some of the horses he recommended and won't give a hoot if you paid scads for them. After dropping you off, I am going to go straight to my cottage. You can tell everyone I have an upset stomach. I'm sure they'll believe you. You're obviously an excellent liar!' she finished, whirling on the heels of her riding boots and stalking off.

Bandar gritted his teeth as he watched her stomp across the lawn, her arms swinging back and forth, her ponytail bouncing up and down.

Never in his life had he been spoken to in such a manner. No one would dare—certainly not a woman!

Why he wanted this impossible creature as much as he did was a complete mystery to him. Not only was Samantha Nelson *not* truly beautiful—she was right about that—she had a tongue laced with acid.

Right from their first meeting she had burned him with her words. Burned and challenged him.

A light suddenly snapped on in Bandar's head. Yes, of course! *That* was the reason behind his unlikely obsession with her. She challenged him.

Challenges had always compelled Bandar. Give him an unbreakable horse and he would go to any lengths to tame it, to have it welcome him as its rider, to have the animal eating out of his hand.

He had never actually found *any* woman a challenge before.

Up till now.

It galled Bandar that Samantha was his first failure with the opposite sex.

She came back into view in the side vision mirror, her body language still full of defiance and defensiveness.

He studied the stubborn set of her mouth, thinking to himself how satisfying it would be to have that mouth soften under his, to have it pleasure him as he liked to be pleasured.

His loins leapt at the image of her totally stripped of her defences as well as her clothes. She had a good body: high, firm breasts, a small waist, long, slender legs.

She would look good naked.

Bandar grimaced at the physical effect his thoughts were having on him. He would have to control his desires for now, or risk potential embarrassment.

But he was not done with this woman. She would be his. It was just a matter of finding out the right approach.

What a pity he had so little time. Less than three weeks and he would have to return to London. He might have to be ruthless.

Of course he was already rather ruthless where western women were concerned. Materialistic creatures, most of them. Always pretending they wanted you for yourself, when underneath it was really your money they wanted.

Was Samantha susceptible to money? he wondered as she wrenched open the door and climbed back into the driver's seat.

She did not look at him. Did not say a single word. Just stabbed the key into the ignition and got going.

The sexual chemistry was still there between them, regardless of how much she wanted to pretend it wasn't. Its pull sizzled through the airwaves, making Bandar suddenly aware of the perfume she was wearing.

She had not been wearing perfume the other night, he recalled. So why was she today?

Because she wanted him to smell it. Wanted him to be attracted to her.

So why had she rejected his advances?

Bandar considered the reasons behind her contrary behaviour all the way back to the stud, her ongoing silence giving him plenty of time to explore various possibilities. Nothing made sense—unless she was of a religious persuasion which precluded sex outside of marriage. That would also explain her outraged reaction to his having three lady-friends.

Somehow, however, having religious beliefs did not seem to match this girl with her acid tongue and prickly manner.

No, the reason had to be more personalised than that. Maybe she had been hurt by some man—some two-timing womaniser who had cheated on her and made her lose confidence in herself as a woman?

Horses who had been badly treated often became sour-tempered and contrary. Like Samantha was.

He was considering this idea when another possibility popped into Bandar's head.

What if she were still a virgin? What if the reality of sleeping with a man simply terrified her?

Bandar glanced across at Samantha's steely face and quickly dismissed this last notion.

No way was this girl terrified of *anything*.

Which left him with what?

He had no idea. All Bandar could be sure of was that she *was* attracted to him. He had felt it more than once.

On his part, he was more than attracted to her. Frankly, he could not think of anything else. Even when he'd been lying in bed the other day, suffering from the most excruciating headache, his mind had been filled with thoughts of her.

He wasn't suffering from a headache now. But his

body was aching. Aching with a need which had plagued mankind since the Garden of Eden.

At another time, in another place, he might have walked away. But not this time. By the end of this month he could very well be dead.

Such thoughts made a man prioritise. It also gave an urgency to his desires. Dead, he would never know what it felt like to hold this woman in his arms, to kiss her contrary mouth into compliance, then make love to her from dusk till dawn.

Bandar suspected that sleeping with this intriguing girl would be an experience such as he had never had before. An experience he wanted whilst he could still seize it.

He spent the rest of the drive home plotting and planning her seduction—a seduction which seemed as difficult as it was desired.

Patience, he told himself. Patience.

Facing imminent death, however, robbed a man of his patience, as well as his conscience. Samantha Nelson was going to become his, no matter what the cost!

CHAPTER SEVEN

TEARS trickled down Samantha's face. Slow, sad, self-disgusted tears.

She was curled up in the corner of the comfy lounge in her cottage, dressed in pink flannelette pyjamas and clasping a mug of hot chocolate in her hands.

The sun had set a couple of hours earlier. The night ahead promised to be chilly, but the combustion heater was pumping out plenty of heat. The television was on, but she wasn't watching it. She was sitting there, thinking what a pathetic creature she was. Full of bluster and bravado on the outside. But inside full of fear. Fear of making a fool of herself. Fear of the most important area of her life as a female.

Being with a man.

The drive home had been dreadful, with Bandar not saying a single word to her. And of course she had returned the favour, her tight-lipped pretence at being offended and outraged lasting till she'd dropped him off and gone straight to her cottage, as she'd said she would. There, she'd swept the phone off the hook, clicked her mobile off, then dived into bed, fully dressed, pulling the bedclothes up over her head in a vain attempt to shut out the world and the pain which had quickly flooded her.

She'd cried herself to sleep and not woken till it was nearly dark, at which point she'd risen, lit the fire, then taken herself into the bathroom for a very long bath and an even longer assessment of why she'd reacted so heatedly and adversely to Bandar's declaration that the attraction between them was mutual.

After all, it should have been welcome news, shouldn't it?

At first, she'd comforted herself with the excuse that what she'd said to him was spot-on. He *hadn't* been overcome with desire for her because she was anything special. He'd wanted sex, and she was the only game in town. No, that wasn't right. She wasn't the only game in town. She was, however, the easiest. Why? Because she'd made it perfectly obvious to this man-of-the-world that she fancied him. Hadn't he caught her practically drooling over him at the dinner table the other night?

And of course he must have noticed the changes she'd made in her appearance today. He'd have smelt her perfume, at least. That would have been very telling to a man of his experience.

Then there'd been her manner towards him during their inspection of the horses. She'd been all smiles and deferential questions. Maybe not sweet, but as close as she would ever get. By the time they'd had lunch together, she couldn't have blamed him for thinking she would be agreeable to a pass or two.

And what had she done?

Snapped and snarled at him like some rabid dog.

Truly, he must be thinking she was crazy!

Which she wasn't. Just a coward.

If only she could go back in time, she would do things differently.

The knock on the front door brought a grimace to Samantha's face. It would be Cleo, for sure. Dear, kind Cleo, worried that she was sick. Once before, when Samantha had been laid up in bed with a bout of flu, Cleo had come down every day with home-made soup and other tempting things to eat.

Samantha put down her mug of no-longer-hot chocolate and uncurled herself, hurriedly wiping her tears away with the back of her hands.

'I'm coming, Cleo,' she called out, when the knock came again on her way to the front door.

It wasn't till she was actually turning the doorknob that it occurred to Samantha that Cleo would have called out to her with her first knock. She would have said, *Hi! It's just me, love.*

Samantha's stomach scrunched into a tight knot when she saw who her caller was. Fate could not have planned a more humiliating scenario.

He was dressed in smart beige trousers and a pale blue crew-necked top, beige leather loafers on his feet, not a hair out of place, his face freshly shaven. And there she was in her bare feet and flannelette PJs, her hair all over the place and her eyes all puffy from crying.

'What…what are you doing here?' she stammered, both her hands coming up to clasp together just under her neck.

His eyes flicked over her from head to toe, their incredulous expression doing nothing to make her feel more comfortable.

'Cleo wanted to bring you some soup before she went into town,' he said, indicating the flask in his hand. 'She and her husband spend every Wednesday evening at some club, it seems. I told her I would do it. I explained that I wanted to personally check on how you were.'

'You walked all this way?' she said, before glancing over his shoulder and seeing the golf cart which Jack used to transport people and luggage from the helipad up to the house. 'Oh, I see,' she mumbled. 'You drove down in the buggy.'

Finding some composure—goodness knew how—she straightened, then reached to take the flask from his hand, holding it in front of her as if it was a protective shield.

'As you can see, I'm fine,' she said somewhat stiffly. 'If you recall, I wasn't really sick.'

He peered at her more closely, the low-wattage globe above the door not providing the best of light. 'You are not fine,' he said, sounding both concerned and surprised. 'You have been weeping.'

'If I have, it's none of your business.'

'I am making it my business,' he said firmly. 'I am coming inside and you are going to tell me why you are so upset.'

'You are *not* coming inside,' she said, denying him entry by standing in the middle of the doorway. Her pride would not let him humiliate her further.

His gaze was unflinching, his wide-legged stance and clenched fists reminding her of a street fighter about to do battle. 'I assure you that I am. If you do not move, I will pick you up and carry you inside with me.'

'You wouldn't dare!' she gasped, her head whirling at the thought.

'You will learn that I would dare to do of lot of things, Samantha,' he said, in a voice which sent shivers running down her spine. 'My time here is limited, and I refuse to waste it playing the gentleman. I know that you want me as much as I want you. I *know* it, Samantha,' he repeated, his eyes giving her no mercy. 'Your words might say one thing, but your eyes say another.'

'You're mad,' she snapped. But it was she who was mad. He was giving her a second chance and she was blowing it again.

'That won't work, Samantha. I can see through this façade you hide behind. It is nothing but a bluff. I am a very good poker player, and I know when my opponent is bluffing. In your heart of hearts, you want me to pick you up and carry you inside. You want me to make love to you till the dawn breaks. You are like an unbroken young horse who fears the saddle and makes a fuss if one is brought near. If I did not know better, I might think you were still a virgin.'

'A *virgin*!' she exclaimed, totally taken aback. 'Where on earth did you get that ridiculous idea?'

From the stupid way you're carrying on, that's where, came the rueful realisation.

But Samantha couldn't seem to stop. She'd been fighting with the opposite sex for far too long. Her bloody-minded attitude was deeply ingrained, and seemingly inescapable.

'*Not* a virgin,' he said, with satisfaction in his handsome face. 'That is good news. If you had been a virgin I would have had a dilemma on my hands. I do not sleep with virgins.'

'Oh, right. He doesn't sleep with virgins. Give the man a medal!'

He smiled. 'You have a saucy tongue. I will enjoy silencing it with mine.'

Samantha sucked in sharply. 'You really have tickets on yourself, don't you?'

He frowned. 'Tickets on myself? Aah, yes. I understand what you are saying. You are right. I do. But you, Samantha, do not have enough tickets on yourself. Yes, I can see the problem more clearly now. I should have seen it earlier. The clues were all there. You think you have no natural beauty, so you also think I could not possibly desire you. You think I just want to use you, like some streetwalker. But you are wrong. I find you incredibly desirable. You have aroused and intrigued me from the start. I want to make love to you more than I have wanted to make love to any woman. Ever!'

Samantha just stared at him, her heart thudding loudly in her chest, her head spinning at the passion in his highly seductive words. It might still be flattery— his claim that he wanted to make love to her more than any woman ever—but she thrilled to it all the same.

'I do not have time to play games,' he went on with fierce intent. 'I strongly suggest you say no *now* if you are still determined to reject me. Because once I touch you it will be way too late.'

She opened her mouth to say no, but nothing came out. It seemed her excited body had finally over-ridden her self-destructive brain.

When he reached to take the flask out of her hands she let him, watching with widening eyes as he tossed it carelessly aside. When he swept her up into his arms she let him do that too. Without struggle. Without protest.

With the decision to remain silent, all that silly defiance and pretence abandoned Samantha, to be replaced by something she had never experienced before, but which she found both delicious and intoxicating.

Surrender.

Her arms found a home around his neck, her head nestling under his chin and a sigh escaping her lips just before they pressed against his throat.

'That is better,' he growled as he carried her inside and kicked the door shut behind them.

Yes, Samantha thought dazedly as she melted into him. Much better.

He stopped in the middle of the hallway, his head turning to the right to glance into her bedroom, then left into the lounge room.

'Your bedroom is too small and cold,' he announced, and headed into the larger, cosier room.

His lowering her to her feet on the rug in the middle of the floor brought Samantha out of her daze somewhat. So did his fingers going to the top button on her pyjamas.

'You should not wear your grandmother's night-clothes,' he chided as his fingers worked their way down the six buttons. 'You should wear satin or silk against this lovely skin of yours.'

By the time he reached the last button, Samantha's state of surrender had started receding, her thoughts turning fearful once more. Okay, so she wasn't a virgin, but she might as well be. She had no idea how to make love. Or how to let herself be made love to. Certainly not by a man as experienced as Bandar. What was she supposed to do? And say?

The truth. She had to tell him the truth.

'Bandar…'

His name came out in the smallest voice, one that vibrated with worry and tension.

He stopped and glanced up into her eyes.

'What is it?' His voice carried impatience. Maybe he thought she was going to tell him to stop.

'I'm not a virgin,' she told him tautly. 'But I'm not very experienced, either.'

He stared at her for a long moment, then smiled—a long, slow, sexy smile. 'Do not worry. I have enough experience for both of us.'

His hands abandoned her top, leaving it hanging undone whilst he cupped her face and brought his mouth down on hers. His kiss was as soft as his lips, sipping at hers till they gasped apart. When his head lifted, a low moan escaped her lungs. Her eyes searched his, awed that he could make her feel like this so quickly: as if she would die if he didn't kiss her again soon.

His mouth lowered once more, this time kissing her top lip only, wetting it with his tongue and nibbling at it with his teeth. He did the same with her bottom lip before his head lifted again. By then her whole mouth felt swollen, both her lips tingling, her body taut and expectant. Her nipples had peaked under her top; her belly and thighs were tight with tension.

His eyes held hers whilst his hands left her chin to trail down her throat, down into the valley between her breasts. Her nipples seemed to harden further in anticipation of being touched, or exposed, her heartbeat quickening further. His head lowered once more to her mouth, his tongue demanding full entry between her lips at the same time as his hands slid into the gaping top and covered her breasts.

Oh!

Being kissed by Bandar was exciting enough; having his palms rotate over her nipples at the same time was close to sensual overload! Her head spun, her back arched, another muffled moan echoed deep in her throat.

His head lifted, his hands dropping away.

'Wait here,' he commanded. 'Do not move. I will only be gone for a few moments.'

She did move, shivering and shaking as a violent shudder rippled all through her.

He was as quick as his promise, returning to the room with the duvet from her bed, spreading it out on the floor in front of the fire before straightening it and smiling ruefully over at her.

'Not the king-sized bed I would prefer,' he said. 'But we should be warm and comfortable enough.'

Samantha didn't think being warm was going to be a problem. She was already on fire.

'Come here,' he said, from where he was standing beside the duvet.

She walked towards him like a robot, her loose pyjama top moving with each step she took, bringing an acute awareness of her near-painful erect nipples. His black eyes raked over her as she approached, his gaze possessive and almost smug.

When she reached him, his hands lifted to stroke her hair back from where some had fallen around her face.

'I like your hair down,' he murmured, bending to kiss her lightly on the mouth once more. 'But I do not like these clothes you are wearing. I am going to remove them. Do not be afraid.'

Afraid? Was it fear sending her heartbeat wild? Or the most incredible excitement?

Samantha sucked in a deep breath when he peeled the top open, then paused to study her naked chest. His gaze was unreadable, giving her no indication if he liked what he was seeing. She had no reason to be ashamed of her body, but who was to say what Bandar liked or preferred? Maybe he was turned on by huge breasts and softly rounded bellies. Maybe he didn't like her well-toned stomach or her B-cup breasts?

After what felt like an eternity, he pushed the top back off her shoulders, releasing it so that it slid down her arms onto the floor. The pyjama pants followed suit, leaving her standing before him nude.

Her shoulders squared under his gaze, her chest rising and falling as he walked around her, looking her over as if she was a slave girl on an auction block.

Samantha found it hard to believe she was doing this. The old Samantha—the one she'd been less than a few minutes ago—would never have tolerated such a scenario. Not even in her fantasies.

This newly surrendered Samantha was totally enthralled with the feelings running through her. She could not get enough of his eyes on her. She would have stayed standing there all night if he'd commanded her to.

He shook his head at her after he'd encircled her for a third, exquisitely thrilling time.

'No natural beauty?' he muttered in dark tones. 'Do

you not own a mirror? If I had a harem, you would take pride of place in it. You are made for a man's pleasure, Samantha. For *my* pleasure,' he added as he swept her up into his arms and laid her down on the duvet, scooping her hair up from the back of her head and spreading it out like a halo.

'Do not move,' he commanded as he straightened. 'And do not close your eyes. I want you to watch me undress.'

She watched, wide-eyed and dry-mouthed, whilst he stripped his blue top up over his head, the action leaving him naked to the waist. He was as beautifully shaped as she had known he would be: broad shoulders tapered down to a slim waist and hips, his stomach was flat and hard, his arms rippled with the lean, strong muscles a rider needed. It was his skin, however, which drew Samantha's eyes the most. The colour of milk chocolate, and with surprisingly little body hair, it had the kind of smooth, silky texture which made you want to touch it.

Samantha wanted to touch it. She wanted to touch him. *All* of him.

She swallowed when his hands went to his trousers, unflicking the waistband. But he didn't undo his zipper, as she'd been anticipating. He stopped and sat down on the lounge, where he kicked off his shoes and pulled off his socks. When he stood up again, his hands hesitated once more on his zipper, his eyes thoughtful as they flicked over to her.

'I presume you are not on the Pill?' he said.

She shook her head. No way could she tell him that she was.

'No matter. I have come prepared,' he said, and pulled a foil rectangle from his trouser pocket.

His presumption that she would come across did not escape Samantha. But she refused to let it bother her. His arrogance and his confidence with women were exactly what she needed. Here was her older, more experienced lover: the one who would teach her all she needed to know. The one who'd force her not to fall back into bad habits.

Already he'd given her self-esteem a huge boost. If he'd seen evidence of her attraction for him in *her* eyes, then she'd seen genuine admiration for her body in his. The way he'd looked at her—was *still* looking at her—made her feel as if she was the most beautiful woman in the world.

It was *his* beauty, however, which soon distracted Samantha from any thought of herself. The removal of his last two items of clothing left him as naked as she was.

Samantha had grown up in a household of men; she had seen quite a few naked male bodies in her time. But she had never encountered one built quite like Bandar.

Perhaps it was his state of arousal which made him seem twice the size of a normal man. Samantha swallowed as she stared at him. He reminded her of a stallion, his impressive phallus rising from its nest of dark curls, reaching up beyond his waist. The head was glistening.

It was wet. As she was wet. She could feel the moisture between her legs, feel her body already preparing itself for him.

By the time he lay down next to her, protection in place, she was trembling.

'How many men have you been with?' he asked, whilst his hands started running up and down her body.

'Not many,' she returned huskily. 'And none like you.' No wonder he didn't sleep with virgins!

His smile reached his eyes. 'Do not flatter me just so you can get me into your bed.'

His wittiness made her smile. 'I never flatter men,' she countered, quite truthfully.

'I can believe that. But perhaps we should not talk. Not till afterwards.'

Samantha quickly realised why all those mares had stood so submissively for him. He had the hands of an angel... Or a devil.

Her body vibrated under his touch, the blood charging round her veins. Finally his head lowered, but not to her mouth this time—to her breasts.

A startled cry punched from her throat when his lips closed over her nipple.

This was something Samantha had never experienced. Her university bedmates hadn't bothered much with foreplay. But she'd often imagined how it might be to have a lover do this.

It was nothing like she'd imagined. Because Bandar seemed to be one of only a small number of men who could do two things at the same time. As he licked and sucked on her breast, his right hand slid between her legs, his thumbpad lightly caressing her, whilst his long fingers slipped inside her.

'Oh!' she cried out.

His head lifted from her breast to cover her mouth, smothering any further cries. His hand continued its delicious torment, his fingers and tongue moving in parallel penetration. His right leg pushed between her knees, easing her legs apart. She could feel his erection against her thigh, feel him begin to move his body rhythmically against hers. It excited her, his moving like that. Everything excited her. But especially his fingers and thumb. The pleasure they evoked became almost unbearable, her belly tightening and her thighs quivering. Suddenly she wanted to struggle, to scream out loud, to express her frustration.

His leg retreated abruptly. So did his mouth, and his hands rolled her over so that her back was to him. Before she could protest, a large palm splayed over her stomach, pressing her back into him, curving her spine and bringing her bottom upwards. She felt his hard body curve around hers, felt him move himself down between her buttocks till he reached where his fingers had been, sliding up inside her with surprising ease.

Samantha sucked in sharply when he rolled her face-down onto the duvet, then scooped her lower half up onto her knees. As she went to lift her upper body onto her hands, he pressed her shoulders back down, and her arms slid out in front of her and her head dropped.

'Keep your head down,' he commanded, when she went to lift it once more. 'You will like it like this. Trust me.'

Trust didn't come into it by that stage. She was his to command; his to position this way and that; his to take as he pleased.

The feeling of utter submission to his will excited Samantha. His hands grasped her hips, holding her firmly whilst he began to rock back and forth inside her, slowly at first, his flesh not withdrawing too far from her before he thrust forward again, burying himself in her to the hilt.

She could hear his heavy breathing. Or was that her own?

The moans were definitely hers.

He stopped at one stage, his hands releasing her hips to run up and down her spine. He bent over her, brushing aside her hair and kissing her neck. No, not kissing, exactly. More like sucking. She cried out when he began to bite her, shuddering with both pain and pleasure. She heard him mutter something she didn't understand.

He grabbed at her hips again and started to thrust, much more roughly. Samantha's nails scraped back and forth across the duvet as the sensations he was creating in her body began to build. Everything inside her grew tighter and tighter. Her muscles stiffened, squeezing Bandar, trying to hold him still. At the same time she craved for him to do it even faster, and harder. Anything to release her from this torment. Soon, she could not bear any more. Her mouth opened to plead, or to protest, when suddenly the first spasm struck.

Samantha had read about orgasms. But reading about them had not prepared her for the reality of the experience. Everything which had been building inside her simply burst, like a dam. The pleasure swept through her in waves, tidal in force to begin with. But gradually they lessened in impact, till the waves lapped quite gently at her, making her sigh with the most amazing feelings of satisfaction and content.

Only when her body become like a millpond did Samantha realise that all awareness of what had been happening with Bandar had ceased from the beginning of her own climax. She had no idea if he had come—had not felt anything but her own blinding pleasure.

His firm grip on her hips remained, but his body had stilled, his breathing heavy and ragged.

When he withdrew abruptly, her lower half collapsed onto the duvet like a house of cards. All her limbs had gone limp; her head was like lead. It took the most enormous effort to turn her face enough to glance over her shoulder at him. He was sitting back on his haunches, his hands gripping his knees. His eyes, when they connected with hers, seemed oddly frustrated.

Her stomach contracted. 'Did I do something wrong?' she asked, rolling over and pulling some of the duvet over her. Maybe he *hadn't* come? How would she know?

'Of course not,' he returned brusquely, his hands lifting to rake his hair back from his forehead. 'If I were a sheikh of the olden days I would buy you at once for my harem.'

'Really?'

'Absolutely. You have the makings of a perfect little love-slave. I want nothing more but to stay here with you for hours. Unfortunately, I have to go back to the house. I can feel a headache coming on. I must take my medication or I will be totally useless tomorrow—which I do not want to be,' he said, his eyes locking with hers. 'I will make love to you more than once next time, Samantha. I promise.'

She shivered under his glittering gaze. And the excitement of his promise.

'Have…have you always suffered from headaches?' she asked as he got to his feet and began scooping up his clothes.

Get FREE BOOKS and a FREE GIFT when you play the...

LAS VEGAS GAME

Just scratch off the gold box with a coin. Then check below to see the gifts you get!

YES! I have scratched off the gold box. Please send me my **2 FREE BOOKS** and **gift for which I qualify.** I understand that I am under no obligation to purchase any books as explained on the back of this card.

306 HDL EFZZ   **106 HDL EFYQ**

FIRST NAME	LAST NAME

ADDRESS

APT.#	CITY

STATE/PROV.	ZIP/POSTAL CODE

(H-P-08/06)

7	**7**	**7**	Worth TWO FREE BOOKS plus a BONUS Mystery Gift!
🍒	🍒	🍒	Worth TWO FREE BOOKS!
🔔	🔔	🔔	TRY AGAIN!

www.eHarlequin.com

Offer limited to one per household and not valid to current Harlequin Presents® subscribers. All orders subject to approval.

◄ DETACH AND MAIL CARD TODAY! ▼

'They are a recent development. I will be all right if I take my medication quickly enough. Now, point me to your bathroom. I must hurry.'

CHAPTER EIGHT

SAMANTHA stayed curled up in the duvet in front of the fire after Bandar had gone. Her body felt totally relaxed, but her mind did not take long to rev up again, finding all sorts of complications.

Just when and where would their affair take place? He could not keep coming down to her cottage. The staff at the stud would cotton on. This was the country, not the big, bad city. Things were quickly noticed here and talked about. The men would lose respect for her and her working life would become very difficult indeed.

Her intention to quit her position at the stud at the end of June made no difference. The horsey world in Australia was not that large. Everyone knew everyone. A good reputation was important. At least it was to Samantha. A lot of the girl grooms slept around, and she'd heard what the men said about them. She couldn't bear to have herself gossiped about that way.

Visiting Bandar up at the main house was out of the question for the same reasons. Staff would see her car parked outside late into the night and start asking questions.

Then there was the problem of Cleo.

Samantha supposed she could tell her about Bandar, and then have Cleo sneak her into Bandar's bedroom without anyone else finding out. But Samantha cringed at that idea. Perhaps because she knew Cleo could never keep a secret. Or probably because she just didn't want to see the incredulous look on Cleo's face.

She still felt somewhat incredulous herself. What was it about her which Bandar liked so much? He'd claimed she'd aroused and intrigued him from the start. Why was that?

The only thing she could think of was that she'd stood up to him a couple of times. Maybe strong women turned him on.

Not that she'd proved all that strong in the end. She'd been like putty in his hands tonight. Samantha shivered at the memory of her total subservience to his will. He'd ordered and she'd obeyed.

He was right. She did have the makings of a perfect little love-slave. For him, anyway. She would have to find some will-power before tomorrow, or she'd be agreeing to move into his bedroom and to hell with what everyone thought!

The morning found Samantha still curled up in the duvet. Great sex sure made a girl sleep soundly, she thought as she yawned and stretched. How fabulous did she feel! This was what she'd been missing all these years. This was what her girlfriends had often raved about.

And why, maybe, some women got mixed up with the wrong men.

Because they were good in bed.

Bandar wasn't just good in bed, Samantha conceded.

He was awesome. And she didn't mean just the way he was built. Though that was pretty fabulous, too.

She shivered at the memory of Bandar's hands. The way they'd touched her. She could not wait to have him touch her again. And look at her again. With no clothes on.

Her thoughts brought a swirling sensation to her head and a tightness to the pit of her stomach.

She was getting turned on, she recognised. 'Get up, girl,' she ordered herself, then immediately thought of Bandar again. He did like to order her around. And she liked to obey. Mindlessly. Blindly. Wantonly.

Her head swirled again, her belly tightening even further.

Her groan was full of frustration. Keeping her mind on her job today was going to be almost impossible. She'd be thinking of Bandar all the time. Looking out for him. Wanting him.

The wanting part would be the most trying. She hadn't realised how quickly desire could strike. One moment she'd been totally relaxed and content. The next, she'd been consumed with the need to be made love to again. She craved another climax. Craved Bandar inside her. Craved the soothing contentment of afterwards.

Jumping to her feet, Samantha swept the duvet up off the floor and hurried from the room.

'I can see you're still not feeling well.'

Samantha frowned as she glanced up at Gerald. They were halfway through worming the mares due to foal in August—an easy, though boring job. No real concentration was needed, and she'd been off on another planet the whole time.

But she could hardly tell Gerald what had been filling her mind. He'd be shocked to the core. Better to be keep Bandar's little white lie going. He'd apparently told them yesterday that she'd had an upset stomach.

'I'm not quite on top of things yet,' she said.

'Stomach still bothering you?'

'Mmm. My head, too.' And wasn't that the truth? Her head was her main problem. It simply would not give her any peace, constantly filling with images of her and Bandar last night.

'You should have the afternoon off,' Gerald advised. 'Have a lie-down.'

Samantha wanted to have a lie-down. But not alone.

Bandar's sudden appearance at the fence of the paddock they were working in startled her. She hadn't seen or heard him. The golf cart he was driving again today didn't make much noise on the gravel. It was the quietest of the vehicles used around the stud.

'Good morning,' he said as he stepped up onto the wooden railing.

Her nerves were instantly ajangle, her nipples hardening under her jumper just at the sight of him.

He was wearing stonewashed grey jeans and a fleecy black top with a zipper down the front. The day was cooler than yesterday, the sun not providing much warmth.

Samantha looked at him and he looked right back, his dark eyes not reflecting anything which had happened between them. Oh, but he was a cool customer!

But then he was a playboy, wasn't he? He had three girlfriends back home. What was she but another little bit on the side? A fill-in. Nothing all that special, despite his flattering words last night. Just someone slightly different to help him pass the time in what he was probably finding quite a dull place to live.

She had to be careful, and not let herself get carried away with this man. He was perfect as a fantasy lover. To actually fall in love with him would be very foolish indeed. She had to keep him in the role of fantasy lover in her head and in her heart. She had to learn everything she could from him, then wave him off at the end of his stay without a single second thought or regret.

Because that was what he would be doing with her. Hadn't he mentioned more than once that his time here was limited?

At the same time, Samantha could not deny that the next three weeks promised to be the most exciting time of her life. It was difficult to keep her head—or her feet—on the ground, the moment she got within calling distance of him.

'How are you feeling today, Samantha?' he asked matter-of-factly.

'She's not too good at all,' Gerald answered for her. 'Her stomach's still upset. I told her to take the afternoon off. Have a lie-down.'

'That sounds like an excellent suggestion. I have just the thing to settle that stomach of yours up at the house,' he said.

His voice and eyes were betraying nothing. But Samantha could hear the wicked irony behind his clever play on words. He was a devil all right: a sexy, devious, conscienceless devil.

'There is also a nice daybed out on the back patio, where it's warm but shady. The perfect place for you to lie down. That cottage Samantha lives in is in a cold spot,' he directed at Gerald. 'I visited her last night, to see how she was, and thought she would be better off up in one of the guestrooms at the main house. But I dared not suggest it.'

Gerald laughed. 'Very wise move. Our Samantha does not take kindly to male suggestions—do you, Sam?'

Samantha's smile was forced. 'That depends on what they're suggesting,' she bit out.

'Now, don't go getting stroppy,' Gerald said. 'Bandar's just being kind. Be a sensible girl and go up to the house with him—get that medicine into you. Then stay and have a rest. Cleo will be there to look after you.'

'Actually, Cleo will not be there to look after you,' Bandar murmured the moment she was seated beside him in the golf cart and Gerald was out of earshot. 'Thursday is her shopping day in town. She has just left. I made sure Norman went with her, so we will have the house to ourselves for at least three hours.'

'You're very sure of yourself, aren't you?' she threw at him. And of me, she added ruefully to herself.

His head turned to frown over at her. 'We are not back to square one, are we, Samantha?'

'No,' she said. 'But please don't presume I will always be at your beck and call. I have my pride, you know.'

He stopped driving, his eyes whipping round to bore into hers. 'You want me to make love to you again, do you not?'

'Yes,' she said.

'Then do not speak to me of pride. Pride is just an excuse for you not to be what you want to be.'

'And what is that?'

'A woman who has finally discovered the pleasures of the flesh and who wants more. Do not deny it,' he swept on before she could say a word. 'I know what I know. Pretence and pride will be your downfall, Samantha, if you let them. It is time to face the truth.'

'The truth?'

'You are a spirited girl, with a good brain and a strong personality. But you like to be controlled in the bedroom. That is nothing to be ashamed of. There are many women who need that kind of liberation before they can truly enjoy sex.'

'But how can being controlled be a liberation?' she asked, confused by his assessment of her sexual preferences. And yet he could possibly be right. She had liked it last night when he'd ordered her around, when he'd directed all the action.

'If you totally surrender yourself to your lover, it frees you of all responsibility for what happens. You don't have to concentrate, or compete. You just lie back and enjoy. If your lover is a good lover—and by that I mean skilled in the erotic arts, but not in any way depraved or cruel—your experiences can be out of this world. You just like your lover to be masterful.'

'What I would like is for you to stop talking about distracting things and start driving again.'

'You want me to get to the house in a hurry?'

'Yes,' she said, shuddering as she accepted she was now even more excited. There was no doubt he was totally corrupting her.

'Then I will go slower,' he said, and reached over to cover her knee with one hand. 'You must learn patience, Samantha. I give the orders; you simply obey. Do I make myself clear?'

'Perfectly.'

'You will do as I say? Always?'

She picked up his hand and put it right back on the wheel. 'In your dreams, Bandar. Last night was fantastic, but I do still have a mind of my own.' Though she suspected it might grow weaker with each passing day in this man's company.

He pursed his lips in disapproval of her defiance. 'I see you have not yet been broken in properly. But it is early days yet.'

'I am not a horse!'

'That is a pity. Horses cannot talk back. We are here,' he said, stopping right in front of the steps. 'Time for your medicine.'

'You are a truly wicked man,' Samantha said as she climbed out. For inside she was literally quaking with desire.

'You bring out my darker side,' he muttered, striding round the cart to where she was standing. 'Come.' He took her hand and drew her up the steps onto the cloistered verandah. The front doors were unlocked, and Bandar led her quickly through the foyer and down the wide hallway of the wing which contained all the bedrooms.

Samantha had been in the main guest suite. Once. Cleo had been cleaning it in preparation for visitors at Christmas time. Samantha had been helping her—not because she'd had to, but because she'd been lonely.

There were three rooms: a bedroom, sitting room and

en-suite bathroom. All were spacious, filled with good-quality country-style furniture and five-star luxuries—from the king-sized bed and the flatscreen television, hooked up to the satellite, to the corner spa bath with its eighteen-carat-gold-plated taps.

'I shall run a bath,' Bandar said, after he'd steered her into the sitting room and left her standing by an elegantly striped sofa.

Samantha winced. 'I smell of horses, I suppose?'

'I like the smell of horses,' he returned smoothly. 'One day we will make love on a horse.'

'Oh…' she said, her mind immediately forming an image of Bandar riding a horse and her, naked, sitting astride his lap, her back to him.

Her hands were holding the reins, because his hands were busy on her bare breasts. He was naked, too, and buried deep inside her, as he'd been last night. The horse was galloping and—

'But not today,' he went on, breaking the spell of her fantasy. 'Today I wish to bathe with you. Then make love to you in a proper bed.'

'Oh,' she said, for a second time. Was there no end to the erotic scenarios he would propose, which he had obviously experienced before?

A black jealousy claimed Samantha as she thought of Bandar bathing with other women, not to mention making love to them on galloping horses, and hard floors, and soft beds, and probably countless other places and positions.

'You've done these things with other women, have you?' she blurted out.

'What? Oh…*other* women.' His dark eyes narrowed, his brows drawing together as he considered his answer.

Samantha's heart grew tight in her chest. She didn't want him to admit it. And what if he said he had? What would she do? Would she have the courage to walk away?

'I have known many women. In fact, I have moved in a very different world to you, Samantha,' he said at last, 'where obscene wealth brings out the worst in men. *And* women. I have witnessed many scenes—most recently at a private party I attended not that long ago—but I was revolted. I enjoy playing erotic games, but lovemaking, for me, is a private and very personal activity. I do confess to preferring a partner who likes me to be master in the bedroom. I am not one of those inadequate men who needs the woman on top, so to speak. It is I who does the riding. I who does the binding.'

'The *binding*?'

'You will like being bound,' he stated, with shocking confidence.

'How can you be sure?' she asked, but breathlessly. The idea was already exciting her, bringing all kinds of questions into her head. How would he tie her up? Where? And for how long?

'I am sure,' he stated firmly, his eyes fixing on her parted lips. 'There are tea and coffee-making facilities over there,' he went on, nodding towards the built-in wall unit, the long wooden doors cleverly concealing everything a person would require to make a drink or a snack. On the day Samantha had been helping Cleo clean, her job had been to fill the small fridge with wine and soft drinks.

'You might like to make us something hot to drink whilst I run that bath.'

'No,' she replied, frustrated by his coolness and his control. 'I don't want a drink. I want you to kiss me. I *need* you to kiss me, Bandar. Right now.'

Bandar was taken aback by her passionate rebellion. But also stirred by it.

This was what had bewitched him about her from the start. Her headstrong spirit. And, yes, her passion. Having her blindly obey him last night had been extremely satisfying, but when she was like this—her blue eyes blazing and that saucy mouth of hers spitting defiance— he wanted to rip the clothes from her body and ravage her on the spot.

'If I kiss you, I might not be able to wait,' he admitted, feeling some alarm at the way he was suddenly feeling—like a volcano about to erupt.

'You're the one talking too much now,' she said. 'Why don't you just shut up and kiss me?'

Bandar's already precarious control snapped.

He covered the ground between them in a split second, crushing her against him and plundering her lips as he had never plundered a woman's mouth before. She more than matched him with her own hunger, her hands grabbing him by his top and yanking him even harder against her.

Bandar knew he could not last much longer, a situation which was quite shocking to him. He prided himself on his skill as a lover. To come prematurely would be mortifying in the extreme.

In desperation, he grabbed her ponytail and yanked her away. Their mouths burst apart, and Bandar stared down into her wildly dilated eyes before he suddenly fell to ripping off her clothes.

To hell with his pride. To hell with everything!

She helped him with the shedding of her jumper over her head, and then with her bra. Her jeans were a temporary stumbling block when the zipper caught in the fraying denim halfway down. He tipped her back onto the nearby sofa and dragged them down her legs, taking her elastic-sided riding boots with them. Her panties followed—unsexy cotton briefs which Bandar vowed to burn.

Once totally naked, she actually jumped to her feet and attacked *his* clothes. Bandar was too stunned—and too turned on—to stop her. She was like a wild animal, ripping and clawing at him. By the time he stood naked also he was once again perilously close to the point of no return.

She should not have touched him—should not have caressed him like that!

He took her standing up, lifting her onto her toes as he rammed up into her. Once anchored deep inside her, he carried her across the room and pushed her up against the wall unit, taking her wrists and pinning her arms wide against the wood, holding her solidly captive whilst he started pounding into her. He heard her cry out, and didn't know if it was a cry of pain or pleasure. He didn't care. He had totally lost it.

Bandar came with a speed unknown to him. Barely ten seconds after penetration he ejaculated, groaning and shuddering like some horny teenager with no control at all. His not using protection made him groan for a different reason. Yet how delicious it felt without anything between them. Bandar wallowed in the sensation of his seed flooding her womb. More satisfaction followed when she came, his physical pleasure heightened as her avid flesh milked him.

True regret was slow in coming. But when it did Bandar squeezed his eyes tightly shut, his lungs expanding then deflating in a deeply troubled breath.

Samantha was going to be furious with him. And rightly so. Though, damn it all, her behaviour had not helped. How could she expect a man to control himself in such a situation?

But you always have before, Bandar, came a rueful voice from deep inside. You never lose control. Never, ever.

Why are you so different with this girl?

A sound escaped her lips: half-sigh, half-sob.

He opened his eyes to find that hers were half closed, her head turned to one side. He got the impression she would sink to the floor if he wasn't still holding her arms up against the wall.

'Are you all right?' he asked, not daring to let her go.

Her eyelids opened slowly. Her smile was just as slow.

'Lovely, thanks,' she murmured.

'I did not use protection,' he said, becoming more perturbed by his reckless stupidity with each passing moment.

He did not want a child—especially not now, when he might not be here to protect it. Material provision could always be made, but having money was not the answer to everything, no matter what some people thought. A child needed his father to be there for him during his growing up years.

'Yes,' she said. 'I did notice that.'

How calm she sounded. *Too* calm. Bandar's gut crunched down hard, his concerns suddenly changing direction. Surely he hadn't just fallen for the oldest trick in the book? Was this what she'd planned all along? To seduce him and trap him with a child?

She would not be the first woman to try this tactic, not by a long shot. He had been almost caught once before, and his close call had made him very careful. This incident was the first slip-up he had made in fifteen years.

Bandar searched her unmade-up face, trying to see the truth behind her seemingly ingenuous persona.

Usually, Bandar could spot a fortune-hunter a mile off. He found it hard to believe Samantha was of that ilk, but no one knew better than he that some women would stop at nothing to get their greedy hands on his family's fortune.

'Why did you not stop me?' he ground out.

Samantha was startled by the anger in his voice. Then annoyed.

'*You* could have stopped,' she pointed out. 'No one forced you to do what you just did.'

His abrupt dropping of her arms and his equally abrupt withdrawal from her body brought a startled cry to her lips.

His eyes narrowed on her till they were cold slits of black ice. 'You are not inexperienced at all, are you? You have deceived me.'

'I have never deceived you,' she declared, but then pulled a face when she thought of her one small deception.

'I can see the guilt in your face.'

His accusatory tone made her mad. 'Just one wretched little white lie,' she threw at him. 'One which should please you.'

'Tell me.'

'I *am* on the Pill. I just didn't want to say.'

Funny. He didn't look pleased.

'I do not believe you,' he said coldly.

'What?' she said, her back straightening as her shoulders pressed against the wall unit.

'You heard me.'

'Yes. I certainly did. It just took a moment or two for the insult to sink in. Now that it has, I have one thing to say to you, Sheikh Bandar bin Bastard. Go to hell. Go straight to hell. And do not under any circumstances ever speak to me again!'

Samantha pushed him out of the way as she lurched away from the wall. 'Unfortunately I have to use your bathroom before I can leave,' she said angrily as she scooped up her clothes. 'Aside from the fact I desperately need to pee, I intend making sure I wash as much of you from me as I can,' she declared. She held her clothes in front of her, her knuckles white with fury. 'Not because there's any possibility of my having your child, you unspeakable excuse for a man, but because I could not bear to walk around with a single reminder that I once gave myself so totally to a man who had no respect for me whatsoever. But then, you don't respect any woman, do you, Bandar?' she finished up, whirling on her heels and stomping off to the bathroom.

CHAPTER NINE

BANDAR sat in thoughtful silence on the sofa, sipping a mug of tea and waiting for Samantha to emerge. She'd been in there for several minutes, during which the shower had been running for some considerable time. He didn't doubt the bathroom door was locked, so he hadn't bothered trying it. There was no point in talking to her whilst she was in such a fury.

Instead, he'd dressed, made some tea, spooned in several spoonfuls of sugar and sat down to drink it.

Her tirade had disturbed him. Had made him question himself in a way that no one had ever made him question himself—especially over his treatment and opinion of women.

His cynicism about the opposite sex, Bandar realised as he sipped, was so deep that it was bordering on paranoid. He understood why that was so. He had just cause for his attitude. But did that make it right?

Not every female in this world was a cold-blooded fortune-hunter, he conceded. Meeting him, however, and finding out he had billions at his disposal invariably brought out the greed in a person. He had seen the women he'd dated change once they realised just how wealthy he was. Suddenly they were willing to do anything for him. That private party he'd been invited to had been thrown by a woman who'd thought he could be seduced by such goings-on. She'd mistakenly imagined he might part with a lot of money to enjoy depravity on a regular basis.

Bandar had stormed out and never spoken to her again.

The three lady-friends he'd told Samantha about were nothing like that. They were, however, exceptions to the rule—all extremely wealthy in their own right, independent and successful women, who had goals other than trapping a rich man into marriage.

His relationships with them were casual and strictly sexual. Samantha seemed to think that was disgusting. But he had never promised or pretended to any of them that she was the only female in his life. They did not seem to mind that they were not exclusive. And they certainly were not in love with him. He provided them with company and sex, and vice versa. If he did not survive his operation next month they would not grieve for too long, if at all.

No one, Bandar had finally accepted, would truly grieve for him. He had no close family, no wife, no children.

Perhaps Ali would grieve a little. But not for too long, either. His life was full and busy, with his wife and children, and this beautiful place. In time, Ali would hardly remember that a man called Bandar had ever existed.

No, that was not true. Ali's son carried his name. He would never be truly forgotten.

This thought actually gave Bandar a jab of pleasure,

and made him see why men set such store by having a child to live on after them.

After them…

Bandar's hands tightened around the mug of tea as another realisation struck.

He did not want to die. Not any more.

Not that he had ever really *wanted* to die. But there had been a part of him which had not been devastated when the English doctor had delivered his dire news, a part of him which had said *yes*, finally an escape from the loneliness of his life, deliverance from the wretched feelings which swamped him every morning on wakening.

Feelings, Bandar conceded with some surprise, which had been strangely absent since his arrival here in Australia.

Was it because of his sexual obsession with this girl? Or the whole change of scene?

'Well, just look at him!'

Bandar's head jerked up at Samantha's strident voice. She was standing there in the doorway which led from the sitting room to the bedroom, her hands on her hips, glowering at him once more. She was fully dressed, her damp hair scraped back from her scrubbed face into a tight ponytail, her blue eyes still sparking at him.

'Oh, please don't get up,' she went on scathingly when he put down his cup. 'Drink your tea. I'm sure I can find my own way back. A good long walk is always excellent for the constitution. And for making decisions—though I've already made the most important one. When you next contact Ali, please tell him that I have quit. I will waive any severance pay for the right to be out of here in the morning.'

Bandar's first reaction was close to panic—a most unusual state of affairs. He never panicked.

Let her go, his brain told him. She is becoming a complication you can do without.

His body, however, felt differently. It still wanted her.

Gradually, his brain began to argue his body's point of view.

If you let her go, how will you get through these next three weeks? She will keep your mind from thinking of death. She will keep you very much in the land of the living.

He had already made plans to take her to Sydney with him for the weekend. Plans which, he finally accepted, he had no intention of changing.

She watched him rise slowly to his feet, saw the wheels already turning in his head. He was going to try and persuade her to stay. She could feel it.

Her hands dropped to her sides and curled into tight fists.

'There is no need for you to do this, Samantha,' he said, in that silky smooth voice of his.

'I can't stay working here,' she told him. 'Not after this. I was going to quit, anyway, at the end of June. I'm just bringing my exit forward.'

'You do not like working here?'

'No. I preferred working in Sydney. But I am not going to tell you why. I know what you're doing. You're trying to get me talking. You think you can change my mind.'

'I hope that I can,' he said softly. 'I hope you will accept my apology. I was wrong not to believe you.'

His saying sorry startled her. For it sounded genuine. He even *looked* sorry.

'My only excuse is that I have long been the target of unscrupulous women. I have developed a suspicious nature. But I have had time to think whilst you were in the bathroom, and I do not believe you had any secret agenda where I am concerned.'

Why, oh, why, did she have to look guilty?

He saw it. She knew he saw it. For he stiffened, his broad shoulders squaring, his black eyes narrowing.

'Are you now admitting to a secret agenda?' he demanded. 'Is that why you're leaving? Because your goal has already been achieved?'

She shook her head violently, annoyed with herself for letting her emotions show in her face. 'No. My goal has *not* been achieved. Look, I didn't really have a secret agenda where you're concerned. Not the kind you're thinking of, anyway.'

'Then what kind *did* you have?'

Samantha groaned. 'Oh, don't make me embarrass myself.'

'You must tell me,' he insisted.

'Look, I wanted you to teach me everything about sex—all right?' she threw at him, her confession sending his eyebrows ceilingwards.

'Not at first,' she raced on. 'At first I just secretly fancied you. You're very fanciable. Surely you must realise that? But I had no idea you fancied me back. I mean…men don't fancy me on the whole. Last night was…well, it was a shock. And a real eye-opener, I can tell you. I'd never had an orgasm before and… Oh, please, don't look at me like that. It's true. I did warn you I was inexperienced. I don't lie, Bandar. Well, not about most things. And you can't blame me for not telling you I was on the Pill. You *do* have a reputation as a playboy, and you openly admitted to having three girl-friends back home. How was I to know what I might have been risking by sleeping with you?'

'Nothing, I can assure you,' he ground out. 'I had a very thorough medical check just before leaving England and it was all clear. Except for a small problem with headaches.'

'Well, that's a relief. And I promise you there won't be any consequences to what happened here today in any way, shape or form.'

'Why are you on the Pill?'

'What?'

'It is a simple question. If you have not been having a regular sex life, why go on the Pill?'

'It's a long story.'

'I am all ears.'

'You still don't believe me, do you?'

Not entirely, Bandar was forced to admit to himself. But that was probably just his cynicism talking.

He was certainly intrigued by her story. Not only intrigued, but excited. She could not have confessed to a better secret agenda. It fitted very well with his plans, and his desires.

At the same time, he could not help feeling a little sceptical. Last night had been her first orgasm? And she was, what? Twenty-six, Cleo had told him. That seemed highly unlikely.

But perhaps it was true.

'I do believe you,' he said, thinking of his own secret agenda. 'I just want to know the reason.'

'Well, that's too bad, because I'm not going to explain myself any further. I'm going now, Bandar. Goodbye.'

'I don't want you to go,' he said, striding round the coffee table to place himself between her and the door.

'What you want no longer matters to me. Now, get out of my way.'

'No.'

'I'll scream.'

He smiled. 'No one will hear you.'

She crossed her arms and glared at him. 'You don't frighten me.'

'Yes. I do.' He came towards her, his hands reaching out to curl over her shoulders. But he did not draw her close. He kept her at an arm's distance, his eyes searching hers. 'Is this what you always do when a man shows interest in you, Samantha? Find some reason to fight with him and then run away? I have apologised. I *do* believe that you are on the Pill. And you do not have to tell me why if you do not want to.'

'I don't want to,' she muttered, but her arms uncrossed and dropped down by her sides.

Clearly her defences were on the wane. Bandar knew it would not be long before she would surrender to him once more. The prospect brought a sense of triumph and a dark pleasure, sending hot blood rushing round his veins. This was what he wanted. What he needed. Craving her constantly made him feel alive.

All he had to do was take control of that craving and everything would be all right.

'But you do still want me to teach you everything I know about sex, do you not?' he asked in a soft, seductive voice.

Her body stiffened, but her eyes showed she was tempted.

'Come now, forget your pride and be honest.'

'I suppose so,' she admitted grudgingly. 'But I don't like all this sneaking around. It makes me tense.'

'I agree. It is not conducive to total relaxation. Which is why I have already ordered Ali's helicopter. It will arrive tomorrow afternoon to take us to Sydney for the weekend. Ali has put his suite at the Regency Hotel at my disposal. I can teach you a lot in a weekend, Samantha. By Sunday you will not be the same girl. You certainly will not want to fight with me.'

Samantha groaned. The devil himself could not have tempted her more powerfully. To be alone with him for a whole weekend in some fancy hotel suite. Talk about fantasies coming true!

'But what am I going to tell everyone? I…I don't want them to know that you and I are…are…you know.'

'We will invent some excuse. You can say you need to go to Sydney to see your family doctor. Hint at some woman's problem that is too private to discuss. You did say you came from Sydney, did you not? Your father and your four brothers live there.'

Samantha frowned. She could not remember telling him that. But maybe she had. 'Yes, they all live in Sydney,' she admitted.

'That is the perfect solution, then. No one will know you are spending the weekend with me. They will think

I am just being kind in giving you a lift. Everyone will assume you are going to stay with your family.'

Samantha could not believe that he had already ordered the helicopter. He'd just presumed—again—that she would go along with whatever he wanted.

'Like I said before,' she said, with exasperation in her voice but adrenaline rocketing through her body, 'you're a wicked man.'

'Not wicked. Determined.'

'Do you always get what you want in life?'

'No,' he said, and smiled a wry smile. 'There are some things you cannot buy.'

'Are you talking about love?'

'Not at all. I can buy love, Samantha.'

'No, you can't. You can buy sex, but not love.'

'You may be right. But I do not want love, and I never have to buy sex. I get it for free.'

'I'm sure you do.'

He laughed, then drew her to him and kissed her, long and hard. By the time his head lifted Samantha had forgotten that she'd resolved less than a few minutes before not to have anything further to do with him. She could fight *him*, but she could not fight the desires he evoked in her—the needs, the all-consuming cravings.

'What time is it?' she asked, her voice husky.

'Just after one.'

'When will—?'

'Cleo and her husband will not be back till three at the earliest.'

'Then we can—'

'Do you really want to learn *everything* about sex,

Samantha? Not just various positions and physical techniques, but the more sophisticated aspects?'

'I guess so,' she said, not sure what he was referring to.

'Remember how I told you on the way up here that you should learn patience? We are about to go away together for the whole weekend, when we will indulge ourselves to the maximum. If we abstain from any further lovemaking today, your pleasure will be all the greater, your orgasms much more intense. The brain is the sexiest organ in the body. Just thinking about sex is sometimes the best foreplay. Do you think about sex much, Samantha?'

'Since I met you, all the time.'

His smile was oh, so sexy. 'I will take that as a compliment. And what do you think about?'

Her face flamed. 'I can't tell you that!'

'But you must. Talking about sex with your lover is even more arousing than thinking about it. Have you ever had phone sex?'

'Bandar, before I met you I'd hardly had sex at all.'

'I still find that amazing. A girl as passionate as you are.'

'My sarcastic tongue puts men off. That's another thing I'd like you to teach me. How to flirt.'

'Flirting is not something that can be taught. It will, however, come more naturally to you once you become confident in the bedroom. Your tongue will soften as your body softens. Come. Sit down on that sofa. I will get you a glass of wine and we will talk.'

'Just talk?' she choked out.

'I might play with you a little,' he said as he walked over to the wall unit and retrieved a half-bottle of wine from the small fridge.

'Oh, no,' she protested. 'No, don't do that. I couldn't stand it.' She plonked herself down on the sofa—a necessary move, given her legs had suddenly gone to jelly.

'You would have to stand it if you were bound.'

Her heart took off at the thought. 'You're not going to do that, are you?'

'No. Not today. But I want you to think about how it would feel to be bound naked to a bed, or a chair, or to whatever piece of furniture was suitable. Of course you would only do this with a lover you totally trusted,' he went on as he opened the wine bottle and poured some into a glass.

'But why would I do it at all?' she asked, somewhat breathlessly. 'I mean…why do you think I would like it?'

'Try to imagine the scenario. Once bound, you are forcibly rendered into a state of delicious helplessness. You cannot stop your lover from touching you. Or from taking you. Or from forcing you to wait. Sometimes he will make you come and come till you have dissolved with desire. At another time, if he is sufficiently skilled, he can take you to the edge of a climax and keep you balanced there for hours. Which one of those scenarios do you prefer, Samantha?' he said, sitting down next to her and holding the glass to her lips.

By now Samantha's mouth felt like parchment and her head was in a total haze. When he tipped the glass, she gulped down a mouthful of the wine, her eyes never leaving his.

He took the glass away, then bent to kiss her.

'Which one?' he whispered against her lips.

'Both,' she returned with a shudder. 'Both.'

* * *

Yes! Bandar thought triumphantly at her admission. She was his.

'You will be my perfect little love-slave for the entire weekend,' he purred as he held the wine glass to her lips once more.

She swallowed another mouthful, her eyes widening on him.

'You won't hurt me, will you?'

'Never!' he exclaimed, shocked that she would even think it. 'If you give me your body, I will give it nothing but pleasure. But you must trust me implicitly.'

He kissed her between mouthfuls of wine till she looked dazed and he was so cruelly aroused he wondered how he would last till the following day himself. Yet his male ego demanded that he did. Hadn't he claimed to her that a good lover was patient and skilled?

'Don't make me wait, Bandar,' she suddenly whispered. 'Take me to bed now. I promise to be your perfect little love-slave for the whole weekend in Sydney. But I can't wait that long. I need you now. I don't know what's wrong with me, but I…I have to have you inside me.'

He groaned. He could not help it. 'You should not say such things to a man.'

'You don't understand. It's like an addiction, this feeling. This longing. Tell me, will it ever go away?'

'Do you want it to go away?' he asked thickly as he scooped her up in his arms and carried her quickly towards the bedroom.

'Yes. No. I don't know. I can't think straight. I just want you to do it to me all the time.'

'I will do my best,' he said, thinking he wasn't much better.

'How long do we have before Cleo gets back?' she asked hoarsely as he lowered her to the bed and began to undress her.

Not long enough, Bandar suspected. 'About an hour and a half.'

'Hurry, then, Bandar,' she urged him. 'Hurry.'

CHAPTER TEN

'YOU know, Samantha, I think Bandar likes you.'

Samantha took a moment to school her face into a perfectly bland mask before looking up from her coffee. 'Oh, come now, Cleo, don't be silly.'

After Cleo had returned from her shopping excursion into town, Bandar had obviously relayed their agreed story, and a worried Cleo had come bolting down to the cottage to see if there was anything seriously wrong. Samantha had allayed her friend's fears by saying she was just having some women's troubles and wanted to see her own lady doctor back in Sydney, claiming that she didn't feel comfortable going to the old fuddy-duddy male doctor in the local town. She'd also added for good measure that it was high time she visited her family.

It had been Cleo who'd insisted on making them both some coffee, clearly because she wanted to sit down and have a good gossip. All Samantha wanted to do was be by herself.

'I'm not being silly,' Cleo insisted. 'I know when a man is interested in a girl. He keeps asking me questions about you.'

Samantha frowned. 'What kind of questions?'

'About your background. Your family.'

'What did you tell him?'

'Nothing much. Just the bare facts about your mum dying when you were born, and how you'd been brought up in a family of blokes.'

'I see,' Samantha said. Which she did. That was how Bandar had found out about her brothers. And probably quite a bit more. Cleo never stopped at just the bare facts.

'He was very concerned about you the other night. Which reminds me, did you like my soup?'

'It was lovely.' Samantha had found it out on the front lawn the following morning, and had it for breakfast. 'Thank you. You're a kind person, Cleo.'

'I try to be.'

'Not many people are these days. It's become a selfish world.'

'Bandar's a kind man.'

'You think so?' Samantha wouldn't have put kindness at the forefront of Bandar's virtues. His kindnesses usually had an ulterior motive.

'Look what he did for Martha Higgins.'

'Who on earth is Martha Higgins?'

'The woman who owns Valleyview Farm. Bandar didn't need to pay her all that money for those mares. Norm was speaking to Trevor, and he said they weren't worth near that much.'

'How on earth did Trevor find out what Bandar paid for them? Did Bandar tell him?'

'Heavens, no. Trevor heard on the grapevine. You know what it's like up here, love. Can't keep a secret in the country. So I asked Bandar about it, and he said that

Ali had told him about Martha's circumstances and he thought she might need a helping hand.'

'He can afford it,' Samantha said, thinking how easy it was for a billionaire to impress people. Bandar only had to start throwing a few million around and everyone thought he was the ant's pants.

'Lots of other wealthy people can afford charitable gestures, too,' Cleo pointed out. 'But they still wouldn't have done what Bandar did. He didn't have to offer you a lift to Sydney either, madam. Stop being so critical of the man. Truly, Samantha, there I was, thinking you liked him.'

'I do like him,' she admitted. 'But that doesn't mean I have to kiss his backside for giving me a ride.'

Cleo laughed. 'Can't imagine you kissing *any* man's backside.'

Samantha smiled a brittle smile. Oh, Cleo. If only you knew. I've already kissed every part of his body! I can't get enough of him, and it's beginning to worry me. What I imagined would be a bold but positive experience is rapidly becoming a dangerous obsession. I've already become his love-slave. No, not his love-slave. Love has nothing to do with what he's doing to me. More his sex-slave.

'Are you excited about going in Ali's helicopter?' Cleo asked.

Samantha had been trying desperately not to think about tomorrow. Because whenever she did she started thinking about what was going to happen, and then other things started happening.

Bandar had been so right when he'd said thinking about sex was one of the best kinds of foreplay. Every time her mind went in that direction her nipples would go hard and she'd get a tight, crampy feeling in the pit of her stomach.

She had it now.

Samantha knew she would toss and turn all night.

'You wouldn't happen to have some sleeping tablets, would you, Cleo?'

'Oh, dear, you really mustn't be feeling well if you want one of those. But, yes, I do have some. Got a script when I was having a bout of insomnia last year. The menopause can do that to you,' she added, and pulled a face. 'What we women have to put up with. Men sure are the lucky ones. But, as they say, it's a man's world.'

Samantha couldn't have agreed more. Even more so if the man was handsome and rich and used to getting everything he wanted. For some weird and wonderful reason Bandar wanted *her* at the moment. Maybe he just couldn't go too long without sex. Or maybe he fancied himself as an erotic tutor. She could see that such a role would appeal to a man who liked the kind of sex that Bandar obviously liked.

The trouble was, she liked the same thing. She'd revelled in his masterful display in the bedroom this afternoon. He'd made mad, passionate love to her at first, face to face, satisfying her need to have him inside her. Afterwards he'd carried her into the shower, where he'd washed her all over, then carried her back to the bed and made love to her with his mouth till she'd been reduced to total mush. Finally, he'd demanded she do the same to him.

Samantha had read about oral sex. But she had never imagined herself doing it. Or liking it so much.

But she could not imagine doing it to any other man. That was the part which was beginning to trouble her. The fact that she couldn't see herself even *wanting* any other man. Not after Bandar.

Samantha hoped this was just because he was such an amazing lover and not anything deeper. The last thing she needed was to fall irrevocably in love with her erotic tutor.

'I suppose you wouldn't want to come up for dinner tonight, would you?' Cleo suggested. 'I'm sure Bandar wouldn't mind.'

Actually, Samantha was pretty sure he *would* mind. He'd stated quite firmly when they'd parted this afternoon that they should not see each other till the helicopter flight the next day.

'You know, I sometimes think that man is lonely,' Cleo added.

This observation struck a raw nerve with Samantha. Because it confirmed what she already knew. Of course Bandar was lonely out here in Australia. He'd had to leave his three girlfriends behind in London, hadn't he? Necessitating his having to find a substitute for his suddenly empty bed. Namely, *her*.

She was just a fill-in. An amusement to alleviate his boredom.

But knowing the truth about Bandar didn't make it any easier for her to resist him. Or to risk disobeying him.

'Thanks for the offer, Cleo, but I think I'd better not eat too much today. Not if I have to go in that helicopter tomorrow. I'll just have some Vegemite toast for tea. But I'll follow you back up to the house right now and get that sleeping tablet.' She stood up immediately.

Cleo got to her feet rather reluctantly.

'Will Bandar be there?' Samantha asked as both women walked out to their respective vehicles.

'Nope. He's out riding that mad stallion of his again. He said he'd have to ride him again tomorrow morning to make sure he behaves over the weekend. Ray told Norm that he's a right handful, that one. They've tried him in a bigger paddock, but he's still full of beans. Ray says he's one of those stallions who doesn't settle properly unless he's going to the breeding barn every day.'

Like his owner, came the rueful thought.

'He'll be right soon, then,' Samantha said drily. 'He's got a full book for the season. Come late August he'll be popping off to the barn several times a day for weeks on end.'

'You know, the way those stallions can keep going like that truly amazes me,' Cleo said as she pulled open her car door. 'Horses are obviously a lot different to humans. In my experience, most men are oncers. Once a month,' she added with a slightly raucous laugh. 'But maybe that's just my poor Norm. I dare say a stud like Bandar can do a bit better than that. See you up at the house, love,' she said, and was off.

Samantha grimaced as she climbed in behind her wheel and turned on the engine.

Cleo was understating things. Bandar could do a *lot* better than once a month; once an hour was more like it. No way was he going to wait till they arrived in Sydney before the sex started again. It would begin in the helicopter. She knew it would. He'd already told her what she was to wear for the flight down. And what not to wear.

She would obey him, of course. That was what sex-slaves did.

They obeyed their masters.

A skirt, he'd ordered. And no underwear. None at all. Not a stitch.

She trembled at the thought.

She could hardly wait!

If Bandar had had a whip he might have given the horse under him a sharp crack. He wanted the stallion to gallop faster. And faster still.

Just as well he didn't have one, Bandar realised, because Smoking Gun had never liked the whip.

He knew it was his own emotions getting the better of him. He was trying to rid himself of *his* testosterone, not the horse's.

The situation with Samantha was getting out of hand. The more he had the girl, the more he wanted her. He kept having to fight for control of his body. Twice this afternoon he'd lost the battle.

He had lost control, and Bandar did not like that.

Hence his mad ride around the racetrack this afternoon. But it didn't seem to be working.

He had to stay away from her for a while.

He would attend to himself, *by* himself, in the shower. Tonight and tomorrow morning. The thought was distasteful, but necessary.

By the time Samantha joined him on that helicopter tomorrow Bandar aimed to have his wayward flesh under control. For how could he enjoy controlling her if he could not control himself?

And that was the name of the game this weekend,

wasn't it? He was the master and she was his eager little love-slave.

His mind filled with the images of all he was planning to show her and do to her.

His groan sounded tortured. But it was a torture born of promised pleasure. His, and hers. Oh, yes, she would enjoy herself this weekend.

He would make sure of that.

CHAPTER ELEVEN

'You look beautiful,' he complimented her as soon as they were alone in the helicopter.

Not as beautiful as you, Samantha wanted to say. But she was having trouble finding her tongue at that moment.

He was dressed in a black suit—not a business suit, or a tuxedo. Far more casual than that. The jacket was single-breasted, with only one button, the trousers loosely but elegantly cut, their waistband slung low on his hips. He'd teamed the suit with a pale grey rollneck which highlighted his dark colouring. The rings were back on his fingers, but not the gold chain he usually wore around his neck. His hair looked longer than on the day they'd first met, falling in glossy waves almost to his shoulders.

She could not take her eyes off him.

He seemed to be similarly taken with her appearance.

Samantha had to confess that she looked her very best, which was only to be expected since her preparations for this weekend had taken her several hours last night and all this morning.

Her hair. Her face. Her body. They had all been

primped and preened over, plucked and perfumed, till she was as perfect as she could be. Her nails were painted, her bikini line ruthlessly waxed to almost nothing, her skin moisturised and her make-up immaculate.

Her clothes had presented a small problem, since her wardrobe consisted mainly of jeans. She'd bought a couple of skirts and dresses for her Gold Coast getaway, but they were all resort-wear, chosen for the warmer climate of Queensland: light, flowery things which didn't have the sophistication she was looking for.

The only skirt in her wardrobe which would remotely do was calf-length and black, with a split up the front to her knee. She'd teamed it with a pair of black knee-high boots she'd had for years but which never really went out of fashion, and a top she *had* bought for her getaway, a soft silky burgundy number, with three-quarter sleeves and a deep cross-over neckline.

She'd thrown her good black leather jacket over her shoulders for the drive up to the heliport and the short walk from where she'd parked her four-by-four on to the helicopter. Even so, she knew she looked very different from what she usually looked like. Cleo's eyes would have popped out of her head if she'd seen her.

Fortunately, Cleo was not there to see her off. Clever Bandar had given her and Norm the weekend off, and they'd left early this morning to go to Port Macquarie and visit Norm's elderly mother. There was only the pilot, and he was a virtual stranger to her.

Bandar had been waiting for her in the helicopter. The pilot had been the one to take her overnight bag, then help her up the steps, and she'd been terrified for a moment that a wind would come and somehow blow up her skirt and he would see she was naked underneath.

But that hadn't happened, and soon she'd been safely inside.

Safe, but instantly intimidated and terrified.

This could not be her, Samantha Nelson, with this stunningly gorgeous man in these amazing surroundings. The interior of Ali's helicopter was fitted out like a luxury loungeroom in an English gentleman's residence, with wood-panelled walls, plush leather seating arrangements and the thickest carpet on the floor.

But it *was* her, standing there without her pants on, breathlessly waiting for Bandar to do wicked things to her.

'I see you have done what I asked,' he murmured, his eyes not leaving hers as he walked slowly towards her.

'How do you know?' she choked out. She still had her leather jacket on.

'A woman moves differently when she is naked underneath her clothes.'

'Yes. Very carefully.'

The hint of a smile played around his sensual mouth. 'But you like it.'

'I can't say that I do. It makes me feel too vulnerable.'

'But deliciously aroused.'

She could not deny it.

'You will be more comfortable without the jacket,' he suggested smoothly.

She winced as he removed her last defence.

Samantha did not have to glance down to know what she looked like. She could feel her breasts swell further, her erect nipples pressing almost painfully against the softness of the silky material.

He took his time draping her jacket over the back of

a chair, each second like an eternity to Samantha. At last he returned to take her arm, his touch sending an electric charge ricocheting throughout her body, making her feel faint with excitement.

'Come,' he invited, and led her over to two cream leather armchairs sitting side by side. They had a small table between them, on which sat two glasses of champagne, plus a long-stemmed crystal vase carrying a single red rose the like of which Samantha had never seen. Its petals were huge and velvety, the red graduating from scarlet to almost black.

'What an unusual rose,' she said as she lowered herself almost gingerly into the first armchair, trying to hold the slit in her skirt together at the same time.

'It is called Carmen,' he replied. 'Named after the character in the opera.'

'It's very…um…'

'Sensual,' he supplied, before she could think of the right word. 'You will note that your chair has seat belts fitted. Here. Take your glass of champagne and I will fasten you in.'

She almost dropped the glass he handed her, her whole body stiffening when he pulled the belt quite firmly across her waist and clicked it in.

'Not too tight?' he murmured, his dark eyes boring into hers.

Samantha swallowed, then shook her head.

For a moment she could have sworn he was going to kiss her. But he didn't. He straightened, then moved over to sit down in the adjacent chair, belting himself in swiftly before picking up a nearby phone and telling the pilot they were ready to leave. Only then did he pick up his own glass of champagne.

'I forgot to ask if you liked champagne,' he said after they'd both had a few sips. 'Do you?'

'I like *this* champagne,' she replied, and took a deeper swallow. Getting tipsy suddenly seemed like a good idea.

'You should. It is the best. Drink up.'

Samantha was doing as she was told when she felt the floor beneath her begin to rise. Her hands automatically tightened around the delicate glass, but their take-off was remarkably smooth, and stunningly silent.

'I can't believe how quiet it is in here,' she said.

'Everything is very well insulated,' Bandar explained. 'And as you can see, there are no windows.'

She hadn't noticed the lack of windows till he said it.

'What a pity. The view from up here today would be magnificent.'

Bandar pressed a switch in the panel built into his chair's armrest and the large television on the adjacent wall immediately came on, showing a news channel. Another flick of a switch and the screen filled with a panoramic view of the countryside below.

'Channel Six is connected to a camera on the underside of the helicopter,' Bandar told her.

'It *is* a good view, but I can't watch it for long or I'll get motion sickness.'

'I do not want you to watch it,' he said, and switched it off. 'I wish to talk to you.'

Samantha could not believe that he was suggesting that again. Didn't he know how she was feeling? How she'd been feeling since she'd woken this morning?

As if she could hardly breathe for wanting him again.

Her life had been turned upside down by the cravings

which continually washed through her. She wanted to kneel before him right now and take him into her mouth. She wanted to shamelessly lift her skirt. She wanted him to look at her and touch her. She wanted him to ravage her body till she found some peace once more.

She'd become a slave—not to him so much, but to her own increasingly dark desires.

'I understand you do not want to talk,' he said. 'You want me to make love to you. And I will, I promise.'

Her face flamed, her body moving restlessly in the chair.

'But first I wish to explain something.'

She did not—could not—speak. She just stared over at him.

'When I was a young man,' he told her, 'I became addicted to sex. I was like a child in a sweet shop, stuffing myself all the time. I had to have release morning, noon and night. When I was around twenty I took an older woman to bed and was promptly told that whilst I was built well I had no idea how to please a woman. I was accused of having no more finesse than a rutting ram.'

Samantha went on staring at him. Why was he telling her this? What did it have to do with the here and now? He had obviously learned plenty of finesse since then. He was the complete fantasy lover. She didn't want him to talk, damn it. She wanted some action!

But it seemed he was determined on telling his story.

'Stung by her criticism, I made it my business to read everything I could on sex and sexual techniques. The *Kama Sutra* was particularly enlightening. I had never thought of such positions before. Have you read it?'

She shook her head.

'I will give you a copy. But even more educational were other, more obscure erotic journals I discovered, written mostly by the Chinese. Chinese husbands understand that satisfying their wives is as important as satisfying themselves. They have become experts in the art of delay. With practise and mind control they can make love to their wives every night for a week without allowing their bodies release. When they do finally allow themselves release, their own pleasure is said to be enhanced a thousandfold.'

He smiled into her stunned face.

'I do not claim to practise that extreme version. But a few hours' delay, I have found, is well worth the effort. It is also an effective technique where one's female partner is concerned—something I discovered when first using bondage on a woman. If I do not touch you till we arrive at the hotel suite in Sydney, by then you will want me to make love to you with a much greater intensity. You will scream in ecstasy when you finally come. Would you not like that, Samantha?'

Samantha just stared at him. Didn't he realise she was at screaming point right now?

'Well, yes, I suppose so. But, no—not really. I mean…it sounds all very well in theory, but I'm not as sophisticated as you are, Bandar. When I said I wanted you to teach me everything about sex, I never imagined this type of way-out thing. Not that it isn't exciting, mind. I'm really looking forward to being your love-slave for the weekend. And I will happily practise this art of delay at some later date. But please, Bandar, if you make me wait right now, I think I will go crazy.'

His low laugh carried both amusement and satisfaction. 'Just as well I anticipated this reaction. You are far too passionate and headstrong for me to totally control just yet. But that is part of your appeal. Very well,' he said, unsnapping his seat belt and standing up. 'But the lovemaking will be of my choosing. I have no intention of undressing. Or of letting you out of that chair. You promised to obey me for the weekend. Are you ready to follow through on that promise?'

'Yes…'

What was he going to do to her? She began to shake inside with nervous anticipation.

He removed the half-empty champagne glass from her numbed hand and then undressed her. Where she sat. First her boots, each one removed slowly as he knelt at her feet. Then came her top, eased out from under the seat belt and then lifted up over her head. And finally her skirt, wriggled down over her hips whilst she raised her bottom an inch or two.

At last she was totally nude, the leather chair feeling cool yet cruelly sensual against her heated skin. The seat belt was snug around her naked waist, keeping her captive in the chair—except of course she could undo it if she wanted to.

But she didn't.

'You're not cold, are you?' he murmured when she shivered.

'No,' she admitted, the word coming out on a choked whisper.

He moved the table between the chairs aside, then walked around the chair as he'd walked around her at the cottage, looking at her, making her cheeks burn and her flesh tingle. He flicked the lever which leant the chair right back, then walked around her again, stopping behind her to finger-comb her hair back over the chair, after which he walked round to the front, where he eased her knees further apart.

Her hands clenched the armrests more tightly when he looked at her down there. She knew she had to be horribly wet. Knew he could see how excited she was.

The feelings which rushed through her at this realisation excited her even more. He would surely touch her there soon. Maybe he would even use his mouth, as he had the previous day. Oh, but he was so good at that.

But he didn't touch her there. Or kiss her there. Instead, he extracted the rose from the vase and started touching her with it, trailing the petals lightly over her skin.

At first just her arms, with long, light, sensual strokes, running from the backs of her hands up to her shoulders.

Several times violent shudders ran all through her.

Her legs were the next objects of his attention, that tormenting rose travelling from her toes to the tops of her thighs, before skimming lightly over the melting flesh in between.

The air became thick around her. Her eyes grew wide. Her mouth fell open.

Right when she thought she might start begging, he moved on to her breasts, trailing the rose back and forth across them. Her spine stiffened against the leather chair, her breasts lifting and her belly tightening. How was she going to bear it?

Not quietly. She gasped every time the rose contacted an aching nipple, then moaned when it didn't. The pleasure of the petals became a two-edged sword.

Because it wasn't enough. She needed more. Quite desperately.

'Bandar…' His name sounded like a plea. Which it was.

He did not reply, just bent to press the whole rose there, right where she wanted him to, crushing the petals against her most sensitive spot.

She splintered apart instantly, her mouth gasping even wider, her knuckles whitening as her back arched and her bottom twisted and turned against the chair. She squeezed her eyes tightly shut as spasm after spasm gripped her flesh, her orgasm more intense and lasting longer than any she'd had so far.

She did not become aware of Bandar not being with her any longer till she finally opened her eyes and found he was gone.

For a few moments her befuddled brain succumbed to panic.

Gone *where*?

But as her breathing slowed down and her mind began to clear she noticed that there were a couple of doors in the wood-panelled walls. Presumably one led to a bathroom. Maybe he was in there.

She was struggling with her seat belt when he emerged from one of the doors, and a wave of embarrassment swept through her when she glanced down and saw the scattering of blood-red petals between her legs. The rest of the rose was nowhere in sight. He had to have taken it with him.

Her fingers fumbled even more at his approach. She could not believe she had just done that, or that Bandar could do what he had without being turned on himself.

Yet he didn't look in any way aroused as he walked towards her. He looked totally in control, of himself and of her.

'Here. Let me,' he said gently, and helped her with the belt. Helped her get dressed as well.

When she was fully clothed he took her into his arms and kissed her, then held her close, stroking her hair at the same time.

'Do not feel embarrassed,' he murmured. 'This is what you have come with me to learn. Embrace the part you have promised to play this weekend, Samantha, and you will discover a side to yourself which you have kept hidden. You have spent far too many years dressing and acting without femininity. It is time to throw off that façade and become the woman you secretly want to be.'

Samantha could not help but find the nonsense in his arguments, glancing up at him with some exasperation in her face.

'Being a love-slave is hardly being a real woman, Bandar. This is all fantasy stuff. You know, I don't think you live in the real world. You are too used to women doing your bidding.'

'And you are too used to doing the arguing,' he returned quite sharply. 'You agreed to obey me this weekend. Are you going back on that agreement?'

'Can I reserve the right to rebel if things get too kinky?'

'I do not do kinky,' he growled.

'You have to be kidding. What do you think that was just now?'

'You think that was kinky?'

'Too right it was.'

'In that case maybe I *do* do kinky,' he conceded.

She swallowed. 'Just not *too* kinky, all right?'

'You have my word.'

Samantha sighed, feeling comforted by his assurance. Although a playboy in his personal life, Bandar still came across as a man of honour. He evoked a lot of terrifying feelings in her, but none of them was fear itself. She believed him when he said he would never hurt her. And she'd believed him when he'd given his word just now. He might not be a saint, but he was a long way from being a devil.

'So what do love-slaves do, besides lie back and enjoy?' she asked with a devilish smile of her own.

'They do everything their lord and master tells them to do. Without question, without hesitation, and *without* argument.'

'Are we talking just sexual things, here, or everything else as well?'

'Absolutely everything. I do realise that will be difficult for you, but I think you will learn a lot from it.'

'And what will *you* learn?'

Her counter-question clearly startled him at first. But then he smiled. 'I will learn to listen to my first instincts in future.'

'Meaning?'

'I knew you were trouble from the first moment we met. I told myself to walk away, but fate conspired against me.'

'How come?'

'No more questions, Love-slave. The weekend has begun in earnest. Sit down and fasten your seat belt. We are about to land.'

CHAPTER TWELVE

BANDAR stood inside the spacious sitting room of Ali's presidential suite and watched her out on the balcony, looking around with an almost naïve delight on her face. Anyone would think she had never been in a hotel before. Or seen Sydney Harbour.

Admittedly, Ali's suite was splendid, even by the most exacting standards. And the view was second to none, enhanced at that moment by the setting sun, its golden rays slanting off the Opera House and highlighting Sydney's famous harbour bridge.

She ran inside and grabbed him by the arm. 'You have to come out here, Bandar, and look at the view. It's absolutely gorgeous!'

'I have seen it before,' he replied, resisting the pull of her hand. Resisting the pull on his heart as well.

'When?' she asked, tipping her head on one side as she glanced up at him.

'A few years back. I stayed here with Ali one weekend. We went to the races together. Which reminds me. We will be going to the races at Randwick tomorrow afternoon. I will take you shopping in the morning for a suitable outfit. And for some other things.'

'What other things?' she asked excitedly.

He adopted a stony face. 'Do not ask questions, Love-slave. Now, go and run us a bath whilst I order some food from Room Service.'

'Shall I unpack your clothes as well?' she asked, doing her best to act and look subservient, but Bandar could see the mischievous gleam in her lovely blue eyes.

'The butler has already done that,' he replied brusquely.

'Oh, yes. The bowing and scraping Antoine. No wonder you're spoilt, Bandar. Having this kind of service all the time. And living in such glamorous surroundings. Just look at this place. I've never stayed in anything as fancy as this.'

'It is acceptable.'

'Acceptable! My goodness, I've never seen furniture like it. Or lamps, or rugs. And what about those paintings on the wall? They're absolutely stunning.'

'They are not originals,' he informed her, glancing at the well-known Renoirs and Picassos.

'Who cares? They still look great.'

He sighed. 'I do not think the role of love-slave suits you, Samantha. Perhaps mistress would be better. Mistresses are allowed to have opinions. And argue with their lovers.'

'Can't I be both?'

Bandar rolled his eyes. 'How can you be both?'

'I could be your mistress out of the bedroom and your love-slave *in* the bedroom. That way you can dress me in designer clothes and shower me with diamonds in public, but still order me around in private.'

'You wish me to shower you with diamonds?' he asked rather coldly. So! It was beginning already—the

changing. An hour or two of sharing his lifestyle and
she was thinking about diamonds!

'Why not? You could give me a racehorse or two
while you're at it. I don't come cheap, you know.'

His teeth clenched down hard in his jaw, his facial
muscles stiffening with disapproval and disappointment. He had honestly thought she was different. He
should have known better.

Her laugh startled him. 'Oh, Bandar, you should see
the look on your face.'

He frowned. 'You were only jesting?'

'What do you think?' she said, still smiling. 'I like
to buy my own things, Bandar. And earn my own
money. With my brains. Not flat on my back. I told you.
This weekend is just fantasy stuff. For me, anyway. You
might do this kind of thing all the time, but it's way out
of my league.'

His relief was still tinged with irritation. He did not
like the way she was always judging him, and making
him feel he had to defend himself. 'I do not do this kind
of thing all the time,' he stated curtly. In fact he could
not remember the last time he'd taken a woman away
with him for the weekend.

She grinned at him. 'Yeah, right. You've got all the
moves down pat, Bandar. That speaks for itself. I'm not
complaining, mind. I love your hoity-toity lord-and-
master routine. It's going to be fun—and you're right.
Quite good for me. I already feel different. More confident, in a weird way. Is a love-slave allowed to feel
confident?' she added, with the most bewitching smile.

His heart lurched in a most alien fashion. This was
not good. Not good at all. She was supposed to be a distraction, not an addiction. Or an obsession.

'Go run that bath,' he ordered sharply. 'Then get in. I will be along shortly.'

'Yes, Master,' she said, her lips twitching. 'Whatever you say, Master.'

The room felt very empty once she was not in it.

Just as your life will be empty when she is not in it.

Bandar scowled. What life? He'd probably be dead soon.

She is better off without you, so don't start complicating things. Besides, you are nothing to her but her sexual tutor. Her fantasy master. She might like you making love to her, but she does not really *like* you, or respect you.

This last thought truly rankled. His male ego was not at all happy with such a thought. He was used to respect.

No, you're used to being bowed and scraped to all the time, like she said. That is not true respect. That is just your money talking.

Sometimes Bandar hated his money. In his recently made will, he'd left all his racehorses to Ali and the rest of his estate to cancer research. But what if he lived? Maybe he should give it all away. Then perhaps he should come back to Australia.

It had been a challenge to win Samantha Nelson's body. It would be a much greater challenge to win her heart. And her respect.

Meanwhile, he could do little to change the present situation.

She wanted him to teach her everything this weekend? That was another challenge. Was he up to it?

Bandar's hand lifted to rub the slight ache which had gathered behind his eyes. In truth, he was not so sure. Suddenly he was feeling very tired.

* * *

Samantha hummed happily as she poured some fragrant bubble bath into the simply huge corner spa.

She'd decided the second she'd stepped out of that incredible helicopter onto the roof of the equally incredible Regency Hotel to put aside any doubts about this weekend and treat it exactly as it was: the fantasy of a lifetime and a simply fabulous adventure.

Everything that had happened so far only confirmed that decision. The personal security man who'd escorted them to this hotel suite. The personal butler who'd been there to greet them. And the suite itself: superstar luxury and then some, including complimentary flowers and fruit and chocolates and champagne— and who knew what else?

If she started taking any of this seriously she'd end up in some funny farm somewhere.

If there was one last lingering fear it was that she might never find this kind of sexual happiness with another man. But Samantha appreciated that sexual happiness wasn't everything in life—though it was difficult to appreciate it right at this moment.

With the bath rapidly filling, Samantha set about stripping off her clothes and trying not to think that shortly she would be lying back, naked, in that water with an equally naked Bandar. She felt thankful for the coverage the bubbles would supply, which was crazy considering that episode on the helicopter.

What did it matter if he could see her body through the water?

Perhaps it had been too long since he'd touched her, she decided as she scooped her hair up with both hands and wrapped it into a knot on top of her head. There was no doubt that once Bandar started making love to her all sense of embarrassment swiftly fled her mind, replaced by a delicious feeling of abandonment.

The bath was finally full, the temperature of the water just right. As Samantha lowered herself down into the fragrant bubbles she wondered just how many other women had run Bandar's bath for him. And obeyed his every command.

A lot, she forced herself to accept. So don't start imagining that you're anything special in his eyes. You are here just for his amusement and entertainment.

'Excellent,' he said as he walked briskly in, taking off his jacket and draping it over one of the many rails in the ultra-spacious bathroom. 'Our evening meal will be delivered in two hours. That gives us time to bathe and relax together before it arrives.'

'Relax together?' she echoed. 'Er…what does that mean?'

'You are asking questions again.' He stripped with amazing speed before slipping down into the water and settling back in the corner opposite her. The spa bath was so huge not even their feet touched. He leant back into the corner, sighing rather wearily, Samantha thought, as he stretched his arms along the sides of the bath.

'You sound tired,' she said.

Her observation brought forth another sigh. 'A little,' he admitted. 'Perhaps I should not have ridden that horse of mine so hard this morning.'

'Why don't I give you a massage after our bath?' she suggested. 'That will make you really relax. You might drift off for a while.'

He laughed. 'Do you really think so? I rather doubt

it. But you tempt me. Do you know how to give a proper massage?'

'I've had enough of them myself to be able to make a good attempt. I used to have a remedial massage once a week during my soccer-playing days.'

'You played *soccer*?'

'Soccer, cricket, and Australian rules football. I had four older brothers and a father who were right into sport. If I hadn't done what they did, I would have been left home alone all the time. No way was my dad ever going to take me to dancing lessons.'

'I see,' he said.

'That's the reason I went on the Pill.'

'Pardon? I do not understand.'

'All that sport and training stripped every ounce of fat from my body. I was so skinny that I was late going into puberty. Even then I only had a period every six months or so. By the time I went to university things had improved somewhat, but I was shockingly irregular. When I did get my period it was very heavy. Too heavy sometimes. After a few embarrassing episodes I went on the Pill. And I've never come off. The doctor said it was good for me. He said that with my physical lifestyle I needed to put some extra oestrogen into my system, so that I don't get osteoporosis when I'm older. A pleasing side effect was that I finally got myself some decent boobs. Decent enough for me, anyway.'

'Your breasts are lovely,' he complimented. 'Your whole body is lovely.'

Why did she blush? He couldn't even see her body.

'That is not flattery, either,' he added. 'I cannot seriously believe that other men have not found you as attractive as I do.'

'There was this man once,' she confessed. 'A man I worked with here in Sydney.'

'And?'

'He said he loved me.'

'And?'

'He was married.'

His eyes darkened. 'Did you sleep with him?'

'No. I told you. Before you, I hadn't had sex in years.'

'Did you want to sleep with him?'

'For a moment or two. But I didn't.'

'Why?'

'I...I didn't believe he really loved me, and I didn't want to be used.'

'Did you love him?'

'I liked him. We'd worked together for some years and we'd become close. But. no, I did not love him.'

'But he was the reason you left Sydney and went to the country to work?' Bandar said, startling her with his intuitive conclusion.

'Well, yes. Yes, you're right. Paul *is* the reason I left Sydney.'

And the reason she wanted to go back?

Bandar stared at her, but she was off in another world, her eyes not registering him. She was thinking about this man, this married man she claimed not to love. He did not believe her.

'How old is he?' he asked, trying not to sound as though he cared.

'Who? Paul? I'm not sure. In his forties, I guess.'

An older man. Possibly very experienced. Did she want to learn all about sex so that she could please this Paul in bed? Had she run away from him because she had no confidence in herself and in her femininity?

'Is he handsome?'

She shrugged her shoulders. 'He's not unattractive.'

So! He *was* handsome!

Bandar had never been jealous of a man before. But he was jealous of this Paul. Blackly, insanely jealous.

'You are not to contact him when you come back to Sydney,' he declared. 'You are not to sleep with him.'

Her head shot up. She was clearly taken aback by his demands. 'I have no intention of doing so.'

'You are not lying to me?'

She blinked, then smiled. 'Would I lie to my lord and master?'

'You are not taking your role seriously,' he snapped. 'You will get out of this bath immediately and have towels ready for me. You are to dry every inch of me. Very thoroughly. Do I make myself clear?'

She nodded.

'You will wear no robe. You will stay naked, and wet. And you will not speak. Is that also clear?'

She opened her mouth, then closed it again before standing up a little shakily and climbing out of the bath.

The dark triumph which washed through Bandar went some way to soothing his jealousy. And his ego.

This Paul might have her respect. But *he* had her obedience.

CHAPTER THIRTEEN

'COME,' he said, and held out his hand to her.

Samantha took it, and Bandar helped her from the taxi onto her feet.

They had come to the races at Randwick racecourse, as he'd said they would. But he had not taken her clothes-shopping this morning; they hadn't woken early enough.

Samantha liked the feel of Bandar's hand around hers. It was such a simple intimacy compared to those they had shared last night, yet it sent tingles running up and down her arm.

'You are very quiet today,' he said as he drew her towards the members' entry gate. 'Is there something wrong?'

Wrong?

That depended on his definition of the word. Was it wrong the way he made her feel, the things he made her do? Was it wrong that she had surrendered herself to him to the extent that she would do even more if he asked her? Was it wrong that the strong-minded, feisty girl she'd always been seemed to have disappeared?

Images flashed into her head: massaging Bandar all

over, kissing him all over, going down on him. She'd fed him afterwards, her own satisfaction deliberately delayed. Then finally he'd made love to her, spoon-fashion, making her cry out loud. Then afterwards he'd used the ties of the complementary bathrobes to secure her hands behind *his* back, keeping her body bound to his whilst he slept.

But she hadn't slept. She hadn't been able to. She'd waited breathlessly for him to wake, her body wanting him instantly when he did. He'd brought her release with his hands this time, making her beg him to untie her. Which he had, eventually. But only to bind her in other ways. Her favourite had been with her wrists wrapped together, then stretched high over her head and attached to the bedhead.

Bandar had been so right. She'd loved the delicious feeling of helplessness, of having no control.

Light had begun to break over the city when she'd finally fallen asleep, not waking till nearly noon.

And now here they were, at the races, with Samantha already wishing that they hadn't come. Usually she loved the races, but the trouble was she loved being alone with Bandar more—much more.

'I'm a little tired,' she told him. A lie. She had never felt more alive.

His laugh was low. 'I can imagine. But I thought we needed a break. At least, I did. Now, let us go inside and see if we can pick a winner.'

He paid their entry, then took her hand again, leading her through the crowds of people and over to the mounting yard, where the runners for the third race were already being saddled up. The horses' coats gleamed in the winter sunshine, testimony to the good work of their grooms. Samantha tried to show an interest in picking out a potential winner, but she could not think of anything but the man by her side.

Did she love him?

Probably.

There had been far too many moments last night when her emotions had been engaged as well as her body. When she'd been massaging him, for instance. She'd felt almost maternal towards him, very caring and protective, which was crazy: he did not need protecting. *She* was the one who needed protection—from him.

Bandar's hand tightening around hers brought her sharply back to the present.

'That man over there is staring at you,' he ground out. 'Do you know him?'

She glanced over and almost died.

'My goodness, it's Paul!' she blurted out.

Bandar's fingers tightened even further around hers. 'The man who loves you?'

'He doesn't,' she denied. 'Not really.'

'He is coming over.'

She had no option but to say hello, then introduce Paul to Bandar. But how?'

'This is…er…Sheikh Bandar,' she told Paul, who was still staring at her in a most embarrassing fashion. 'He's a friend of Prince Ali—Prince Ali of Dubar. My boss,' she added unnecessarily. Because Paul knew where she'd gone to work, Samantha having had to let him know a forwarding address for tax reasons. He'd even written to her there once, warning her of Prince Ali's reputation with women.

'I have heard of the Sheikh,' Paul said stiffly, and held out his hand towards Bandar, his eyes finally leaving Samantha.

Bandar did not let Samantha's hand go, and Paul's hand dropped back to his side.

'And I have heard of you,' Bandar returned, in that haughty manner he could so easily adopt.

'You've changed your hair,' Paul said to Samantha, ignoring Bandar, who was looking more furious with each passing second. 'Being blonde suits you. It's a lot softer.'

'I like it,' she said.

Seeing the two men together brought home to Samantha why she was so besotted with Bandar. Paul was an attractive man. But Bandar was a man amongst men. A superb male animal in every way. Beautiful and fit and proud, and if she wasn't mistaken he was something else at that moment which made her heart sing.

He was jealous!

'Actually, I've never seen you looking so good,' Paul went on, his eyes raking over Samantha again from top to toe.

Still, his staring pleased her. Because it wasn't pleasing Bandar.

'Are you staying in Sydney for the weekend?' Paul continued. 'Maybe we could meet up for a drink somewhere.'

'Samantha is with me,' Bandar snapped.

Paul looked flustered. 'Hey, I didn't mean anything by it. We're just old friends, aren't we, Samantha? No harm in having a drink together.'

'I beg to differ,' Bandar growled. 'Come, Samantha.'

Samantha threw Paul a slightly apologetic smile over

her shoulder as Bandar practically dragged her away in the direction of the grandstand. One part of her found his proprietorial attitude flattering. But there was still enough of the old Samantha left to resent such high-handed behaviour.

'Hey, cut out the caveman stuff!' she said, wrenching her hand away from his bruising fingers. 'You're hurting me. I seem to recall you said you would never hurt me.'

He swung round and glared at her. 'When a woman is with me, she does not try to organise assignations with other men. You can at least wait until I go back to London. Then you can come back to Sydney and sleep with that fool all you like.'

'What's got into you? Have you lost your brains? I told you. I do *not* love Paul and he doesn't love me.'

'He wants you. I can see it in his eyes.'

'Half the women here today want *you*, Bandar. Do you see me carrying on like some jealous idiot? I am with you because I choose to be with you. If I'd wanted to be with Paul, I could have chosen him. But I didn't.'

That shut him up.

His hands lifted to rake through his hair, his eyes showing genuine regret. And something else which evoked a worried response from her.

The penny dropped. It was pain she'd glimpsed—physical pain.

'Do you have one of your headaches coming on?'

Her question clearly surprised him. 'How did you know?'

'I saw it in your eyes. Do you have some of your tablets with you.'

'No,' he admitted with a grimace.

'Then we'll have to go back to the hotel.'

'*I* will have to go back. You can stay if you want to.'

'I don't want to stay. Come on,' she said, and this time it was Samantha who took *his* hand, Samantha who did the ordering and he the obeying.

Possibly it was the pain which made him so compliant. He did not say a word during the taxi ride, but she knew he was suffering. Once back in the hotel suite, she undressed him down to his underpants, then sat him on the side of the bed whilst she went to get a glass of water. He was fumbling with his bottle of tablets when she returned.

'How many?' she asked as she took the bottle from him.

'Two,' he replied with a shaky sigh.

She took two out, handing them to him along with the glass of water, before putting the bottle back on the bedside chest.

He winced as he swallowed them, a muffled moan escaping his lips as he lay back on the bed and closed his eyes. She hurried over and drew the heavy curtains, then closed the doors so that the room was almost dark. Kicking off her boots, she lay down next to him and stroked his head softly till finally, after an interminable period of time, he drifted off to sleep.

Only then did she take the bottle of tablets out into the light of the sitting room and really look at them.

'Good God,' she gasped. 'Morphine!'

What idiot doctor had prescribed *morphine* for migraines?

Unless it wasn't migraines Bandar was suffering from.

Samantha's heart stopped. No, it wasn't possible. He couldn't have anything more serious wrong with him. He was way too healthy-looking, too strong and too virile.

Look at the way he had ridden Smoking Gun around that track. Would a sick man do that? Okay, so it had made him tired. She'd be tired, too.

And yet what about that first night over dinner? Had it just been jet lag he'd been suffering from? Or had he been suddenly struck down by one of these simply appalling headaches?

He'd had another one on Wednesday night, too. Now another, only a few days later.

She knew migraines could be very bad, but usually not this frequent. And why have morphine to treat them?

She tiptoed back into the bedroom, placing the bottle of tablets by the bed before lying back down next to Bandar. He was breathing deeply now, his face free from pain. He did not stir when she kissed him lightly on the forehead, did not see the tears which filled her eyes and trickled down her cheeks.

'You have to be all right,' she whispered. 'You *have* to be.'

Bandar woke to find Samantha sound asleep by his side, fully clothed. His head still felt thick, but that was probably the after-effect of the tablets. He picked up her hand, which was lying across his chest, lifted it to his mouth and kissed it.

She stirred immediately, her eyelids fluttering open.

'You're awake,' she said, and he smiled over at her.

'So are you.'

'How do you feel?' she asked, her eyes searching his face.

'Much better, thanks to you,' he said, sucking one of her fingertips into his mouth, then turning her hand over and licking the centre of the palm. She gasped and tried to pull her hand away, but he grabbed her wrist with his other hand and she stopped struggling.

'You make almost as good a nurse as a love-slave,' he murmured, then licked her palm again.

Keep it light, Bandar, he told himself, and sexy. This is all she wants from you for now.

But he had hopes for the future. If he *had* a future.

'Bandar...'

'What?'

'You don't have a brain tumour, do you?'

He could not help it. Surprise stopped him in mid-lick, his head jerking up to meet her far too intelligent eyes.

'Do not lie to me,' she said almost sternly.

What did she think he was? A total fool? If he told her the truth then this was over, right now. He *had* to lie. Because he could not leave her just yet. He loved her too much.

At the same time, Bandar accepted that it was insane to delay his operation much longer. For one thing, he could not bear any more of these headaches. They were crippling; only his male pride had stopped him from screaming with pain this afternoon. He would contact Ali by e-mail later this evening and explain the situation. He'd brought his laptop with him. He'd e-mail his surgeon's office as well. And then he would book a seat on a flight to London for tomorrow night.

The next twenty-four hours, however, were going to be his. With the woman he loved.

'Where on earth did you get that idea?' he said.

'The tablets—they're morphine. You don't take

morphine for migraines. You do, however, take them for cancer.'

'Cancer!' He'd never actually thought of his brain tumour in that way. But it *was* cancer, of course.

The word was sobering. It was also very effective at making people look at you differently. If he confessed he had cancer she would be too afraid to have him make love to her.

'Do I look like I have cancer?'

'No…'

'I suffer from headaches,' he said. 'Flying always brings them on. I have found morphine to be the most effective medication. Those tablets are not strong ones, I assure you. I am not an addict. The only thing I am addicted to is you, my darling. Now, where was I?' he murmured, and returned to licking her hand.

She stopped questioning him, her eyes gradually glazing over.

He undressed her slowly, tenderly, taking his time to kiss every part of her body, to imprint the memory of her sighs on his mind. She would be the last thing he would think of before he went into that operating theatre. If he died, he would go with a smile on his face and love in his heart.

CHAPTER FOURTEEN

SAMANTHA didn't want to go back. As the time for their departure approached, her joy began to dim and her mood darkened.

So, it seemed, did Bandar's.

At four, neither of them made any move to get up and get dressed. Yet the helicopter was booked to leave at five, so that they could get home before dark.

Not that the stud felt like home any more to Samantha. *This* was where she was at home: in bed with Bandar.

'Don't go,' she said when he finally went to rise, her hands reaching out to clasp his arm.

When he turned, his face was grim. 'We cannot stay here for ever, Samantha. As much as I would like to.'

'Would you really?'

He bent to kiss her lightly on the lips. 'Of course I would. But life goes on. I have things I must do.'

'But you're not really needed back at the stud,' she argued. 'And neither am I. I could quit. We could go away together somewhere. Or we could stay here. For a while at least.'

His smile was strangely sad. 'You must not tempt me. Like I said, I have things I must do. And they aren't back at Ali's stud. There has been an emergency at home. I have to return to London tonight.'

Her stomach felt as if it had suddenly fallen into an abyss. 'You're going back to London?'

'I have to.'

'But…but why?'

'It is a private matter.'

'Take me with you,' she begged, panic spreading through her whole body.

'I am sorry, but I cannot.'

Her panic gave way to desolation… Desolation and desperation.

'But I can't live without you,' she sobbed. 'Don't you know that? I…I need you. You must take me with you. I won't be a bother, I promise. You can have those other women if you want, as long as you have me as well. Oh!' she cried, her whole mind shattering apart at the humiliating reality of what she'd just said.

She buried her face in her hands and wept.

His arms around her were gentle. 'I am not going back to those other women,' he said softly as he cradled her against his chest. 'I will come back to you as soon as I can.'

His amazing words brought some hope to her heart. Her eyes lifted, still glistening with tears. 'You mean that? You'll come back?'

He smiled and kissed her on the forehead. 'Would I abandon my perfect little love-slave?'

'When? When will you come back?'

'As soon as I can.'

'But when is that?'

'I'm not sure how long it will take to attend to this emergency. Be assured, I will not delay my return. If and when everything is fixed.'

'You don't sound sure that this problem can be fixed. Is it money? Have you run into trouble with some investments? Look, I don't care if you're poor. Please don't ever think that. I don't give a hoot about your money. I have money. I can pay for you to come back. I can support you.'

He stroked her hair and smiled so sweetly at her. 'This is not a matter of money. Now, do not upset yourself further. Go back in the helicopter and I will be in contact shortly. I will take your phone number with me.'

'You promise?'

'I promise.'

'When?'

'Give me a few days.'

Bandar could see she was not happy with that. But he could not risk talking to her when his emotions would be fragile. He had to stay strong for his operation. Had to change his will as well. In a few days she would be contacted. Either by him or his lawyer. For he aimed to leave her everything he owned, this woman who loved him for himself and not his money.

'I love you, Bandar,' she choked out, and it almost broke him.

'I'm sure you think you do,' he returned, hating the hurt look on her face but knowing he was doing the right thing.

'You don't believe in love, do you?' she threw at him. 'If and when you come back, it'll just be for the sex.'

He had to harden his heart. Had to find the steel to leave her.

'Would you rather I did not return?'

Suddenly she was back, the angry woman he'd first met, her spirit undaunted, her fire unextinguished.

'Please yourself,' she snapped. 'You always do.'

He smiled. 'I am glad to see that you have not changed. You still have more character than any woman I have ever known. You will see me again, Samantha, *insh'allah*.'

Samantha cried the whole way back in the helicopter. Character? She didn't have any character. She was a total mess!

She was still crying as she stumbled down the steps of the helicopter and threw herself into the arms of the red-haired woman standing at the bottom of the ladder.

'What's this all about?' Cleo asked, obviously perplexed. 'What's happened? Dear heavens, there's not anything seriously wrong with you, is there?'

'I...I can't tell you here.'

'Okay. I'll get your case and we'll go to the house. But where's Bandar?'

'On his way to London, the bastard,' Samantha blurted out.

Cleo's eyebrows shot up, but she didn't say anything, wise woman that she was. She waited till they were alone in the kitchen of the main house, with a cup of soothing coffee sitting in front of Samantha. The helicopter had long gone, and everything was very quiet.

'You've been sleeping with him, haven't you?' Cleo said, straight out.

Samantha was way past denying it, so she just nodded.

'When did all this start?'

'Last Wednesday night,' Samantha said with a weary sigh. Now that she'd stopped crying she just felt terribly tired. Though it was more an emotional than a physical tiredness.

'Mmm. The night I gave him that soup to bring to you. He's a fast mover; I'll give him that. And of course you haven't been sick, have you? That was all an invention.'

'I'm sorry, Cleo.'

'Don't be. I'd probably have done the same thing in your boots. Hard to knock back a man like that. I knew he liked you. I told you. By the way, why's he gone back to London?'

'He said there was some sort of emergency. He wouldn't tell me what. It sounded a bit suspect to me. He said he'd e-mailed Ali and explained the situation.'

'I'll give Ali a call later. He'll tell me what's up. So what's our playboy like in bed? Devastatingly good, by the look of you.'

'I can't begin to describe it.' If she did, Cleo would probably faint dead away.

'I suppose you've fallen in love with him?'

'Unfortunately.'

'Oh, I don't know about that. Sometimes it's better to have loved and lost than never to have loved at all.'

'That's crap, Cleo, and you know it.'

'But at least you've experienced the very best. Not a lot of women have, you know.'

'He was a fantasy come true. Maybe I should have kept remembering the fantasy part, then I might have kept my head.'

'He's one sexy man, all right.'

'He said he'd come back.'

'Really? You forgot to mention that bit.'

Samantha pulled a face. 'I don't believe him. He's gone and he's never coming back. He just said that to shut me up.'

'Really? Bandar doesn't strike me as a liar. I think I'll go and give Ali that call—see what I can find out about this so-called emergency back in London. Wait here.'

'I'm not going anywhere,' Samantha said wretchedly.

Cleo was gone quite a while, leaving Samantha too much time by herself to think, and to relive that last incredible night with Bandar. He'd been so different with her—not at all dominating or demanding, but a tender lover. She'd adored him that way perhaps even more than she had when he'd been doing his lord and master act. They'd talked, too: not about sex, but horses, mostly, and their mutual passion for them.

They hadn't spent every second in bed, either. They'd relaxed over a lovely meal at the dining table, then sat together out on the balcony with a glass of cognac afterwards, soaking up the glorious view and each other's company. She'd felt so happy. So...loved?

'I can't believe it,' Cleo said as she hurried back into the kitchen, snapping Samantha out of her dreaming. 'He looked so well.'

Samantha's stomach contracted fiercely.

'Oh, no!' she exclaimed as she jumped to her feet. 'He *has* got a brain tumour, hasn't he?'

She saw the horrific truth in Cleo's eyes. 'How on earth did you know?'

Samantha dashed for the nearest toilet, where she retched into the bowl. Retched and retched.

By the time she emerged she felt totally drained, but she'd come to a decision.

'Tell me what Ali said,' she demanded of Cleo. 'Tell me everything.'

Everything was not much. Men were not the world's greatest communicators. Bandar had a malignant brain tumour—operable, but highly risky. He'd delayed his operation to come out to Australia because Ali had asked him to. He'd felt obligated because Ali had once saved his life. It was an Arab thing. Not that Ali had agreed with him.

'Apparently, Ali told him a couple of nights back to get his butt back to London, *pronto*,' Cleo continued. 'Before things got worse. Because everyone knows things always get worse with cancer.'

'A couple of nights ago?' Samantha queried. 'Not yesterday?'

'No. Ali said Saturday.'

Samantha could have cried with both joy and despair. Bandar had stayed with her another night. He hadn't wanted to leave her. He loved her. He must! Why else would he not have told her the truth? He was protecting her. Or was it that he just didn't believe she truly loved him?

What did it matter *what* he believed? She had to go to him. Be with him. Show him how much she cared.

But maybe it was already too late.

'When is this operation due, do you know?'

'As soon as it can be scheduled. That's all Ali knows. What are you going to do?'

'I'm flying to England. I'll go get my passport, then drive to Sydney tonight and catch the first plane available. Can you get some information from Ali for me? I need to know Bandar's address in London, and the hospital where he's being treated. Don't let him tell Bandar. I'll ring you from the airport.' She was already up and off, adrenaline revving up her energy level.

Dear God, please don't let Bandar die, she prayed as she ran for the door. Allah, save him!

'Are you sure you want to do this, Samantha?' Cleo called out as she ran after her.

'Absolutely!'

CHAPTER FIFTEEN

SHE was too late.

She could not get a seat on a plane bound for London that night, or the next morning. The first available flight was the following afternoon, and even then she had to pay a business class fare.

By the time the plane touched down at Heathrow Airport, Bandar was already being prepared for surgery. Not that Samantha knew that at that precise moment. She didn't find out till she reached the hospital, the name of which Ali had supplied to Cleo.

The Sheikh *was* a patient, she was told by the woman on the reception desk. But he was currently in surgery.

Samantha would have asked more questions if she hadn't promptly fainted.

Consciousness returned and she found someone dressed mainly in white hovering over her. Not a nurse or a doctor, but a dark-eyed, olive-skinned man with a solicitous look on his handsome face and wearing a *kaffiah*, the traditional Arab headdress.

Her employer: Prince Ali of Dubar.

'Ali!' she gasped, and sat up abruptly from where she'd been lying on a lounge in someone's office.

He pressed her firmly but gently back down into a prone position. 'Not a good idea to get up too quickly after fainting,' he said. 'One of the nurses is bringing you some tea and biscuits.'

'But...but what are you doing here?' she asked. 'You're supposed to be in Dubar, attending your brother's coronation.'

'The official coronation day is not till tomorrow. By then I will be back in Dubar and no one will be any the wiser. I decided that today my place was with my friend. Unfortunately I was too late to see Bandar before his operation. I gather the same applies to you.'

The reality of why Samantha had fainted rushed back to her, turning her stomach over and making her chest feel tight.

'Oh, Ali, what if he dies?' she cried.

'Then he dies,' Ali returned, far too pragmatically for Samantha. 'What is written is written.'

'I can't stand it when people say things like that. There is no such thing as fate, or destiny. What is written is what you make happen yourself.' She sat up abruptly, not able to lie down any longer.

'He did not give himself the cancer,' Ali pointed out.

'How do you know? Cleo said Bandar is a lonely man. Loneliness can sometimes weaken the immune system. I've read about it.'

'Why would you read about such a subject? Because *you* are lonely?'

'Yes. Yes, I'm lonely,' she said, levering herself up onto her feet. 'I've always been lonely. Or I was till I met Bandar. I love him, Ali, more than words can say. And I think he loves me.'

'I am sure he does. Do you know he has left you everything in his will?'

Shock and grief made her angry. 'Good grief, I don't want his damned money! I just want him alive and well.'

'He knows that.'

'How long does this operation go on for?' she asked despairingly as she began to pace around the room.

'Not much longer, I am told. I asked that the surgeon visit us here as soon as it is over. Ahh, here is the tea…'

A nurse bustled in with a tray. Ali waved her off when she started fussing, saying he would attend to the pouring.

Which he did.

A watery smile broke through Samantha's misery as she accepted the mug of tea he fixed for her. He was just like Bandar. So sure of himself. So much in command of things.

But was she right? Did Bandar's surface confidence hide an inner loneliness?

'Tell me about Bandar, Ali. I need to know everything.'

Ali's laugh was rueful. 'You sound just like my wife, Charmaine. She has to know everything.'

'Tell me.'

'I can only tell you what I know. There will be some things only Bandar knows. Men always have their little secrets, some best kept from the women in their lives.'

'If you mean the three lady-friends he has been entertaining of late, then I know all about them. They're irrelevant.'

Ali's eyebrows lifted. 'I see you *do* understand Bandar. But be assured that those ladies meant nothing to him. No woman has meant anything to Bandar. Till you came along. Not even his own mother.'

'He did not love his mother?' What kind of child did not love their mother?

'She did not love him. He was a ticket to the good life, that is all. She met Bandar's father when he was most susceptible to her kind of beauty and bedroom skills. His first wife—a woman from his own culture—had not long died whilst pregnant with their first child. He'd taken it hard. It had been a true love-match. He went crazy with grief, using his money to try to forget. He went to London to live, and started mixing with a very fast crowd. Bandar's mother was a good-time girl, though the media kindly called her a social-ite. She was little better than a whore, selling herself to whatever man could afford to pay for her very expensive habits.'

'She took drugs?'

'She was not an addict. But she used designer drugs to enhance her promiscuous lifestyle, and to seduce men like Bandar's father, who was not used to such women. Naturally he married her when she announced she was pregnant. By then he was obsessed with the woman. She continued to hold sway over him after Bandar was born. The boy was left to the care of others whilst they swanned off to the world's pleasure spots, spending money at casinos and on racehorses, sinking further and further into depravity. If Bandar's father had not had a continuous stream of money from the oil wells he'd inherited from his Bedouin father, he would have been bankrupt many times over. Bandar's parents were never there for him. They were killed in a fire on a yacht on Bandar's sixteenth birthday. He was at school in London. They were in the Caribbean.'

'What a terrible story. Poor Bandar.'

'Yes. Poor Bandar.'

'How long have you known him? I heard you were friends as children.'

'I first met Bandar when we were sent to the same school in Dubar. I was fourteen. He was a couple of years younger than me. A shy child, if you can believe that.'

Yes. She could. He'd not been wanted any more than she had been. Samantha knew only too well how that affected a child. But he probably hadn't been shy so much as introverted, relying on himself for company, not trusting others.

'The other boys at school knew about his mother. They taunted him about her. Called her a whore. He took it for a while, then one day he fought back. Unfortunately, he chose the wrong group of boys to fight. They were much bigger, and meaner. One was carrying a knife. Bandar had already been stabbed before when I intervened. Fortunately, his wound was not life threatening. After that, his father shipped him off to a Christian school in England. You can imagine what that move was like for Bandar. For a long time he was like a fish out of water. Spurned and isolated by the English boys. Eventually, however, he was assimilated into their world, though he credits his money for finally gaining him acceptance.'

'He's a cynic about his money,' Samantha said.

'Yes,' Ali agreed. 'But he has just cause. You do not know what it is like to be an extremely wealthy man, Samantha.'

'Bandar told me women target him all the time.'

'Some will lie and cheat to unbelievable levels. When Bandar was around nineteen he was seduced by a very beautiful and very clever woman. When she claimed she was pregnant, Bandar was beside himself. She did not want marriage, just money. Lots of it. Bandar, however, did not like to think of any child of his being raised without a father to protect it. Luckily, he spoke to me about the situation, and I had the woman investigated. It turned out she was already married. It was clearly all a scam to get money. I advised Bandar to get a court order demanding she have a DNA test after the baby was born, and suddenly there was no baby. Though there had been one. Whose it was, we will never know.'

'Bandar must have been devastated.'

'He learned a very valuable lesson. From then on he was very careful.'

Samantha could understand Bandar's cynicism, and his wariness, but in the end you had to have some faith in people or life wasn't worth living.

'If Bandar was sent to England to school and to live, Ali,' she asked, trying to piece things together, 'then how did you keep up your friendship?'

'Through horses. We didn't see each other for some years, but met up again when I was sent to my father's stables in England for a short time.'

'I see.'

It was good to finally understand the man she loved. But what good was understanding him if he died? Emotion welled up in her chest, tears filling her eyes. She put down her mug of tea and surreptitiously wiped them away, not wanting to cry in front of Ali.

'It is all right to cry,' he said gently. 'Charmaine cries all the time.'

'Oh, Ali…' She sank into his outstretched arms and wept and wept.

Her tears had subsided to just the occasional sob when the door opened and Bandar's surgeon entered. He was an extremely tall man, with a pleasant face and receding brown hair. He looked tired, but pleased.

'Everything went very well,' he announced straight away, and Samantha burst into tears again.

'His fiancée,' she heard Ali say, by way of explanation.

'But he said he had no one!'

'He kept his condition a secret from Samantha so that she would not worry.'

'Aah. I did wonder. Such an impressive man. My secretary will be devastated. She was charmed by the Sheikh when he came to me for his consultation. But back to the matter at hand: I was able to get all the cancer. It will not come back. His brain is fine, and no nerves were damaged. There will not be any after-effects. I did a brilliant job, if I say so myself.'

'I thank you,' Ali said sincerely. 'And so will Samantha. When she can.'

Overhearing this conversation forced Samantha to pull herself together.

'I can't thank you enough,' she said, grabbing the surgeon's hands and shaking them vigorously. 'You are more than brilliant.'

The man's smile showed some smugness. But he had a right to be smug, in Samantha's opinion. How brave they were, brain surgeons. Brave *and* brilliant.

'Your fiancé is in Recovery, young lady,' he said,

patting her hands. 'He'll be groggy for quite a while. Take it easy with him today. Don't tire him with too much chatter. Or too many kisses,' he added with a cheeky wink. 'We don't want him to expire from too much excitement too soon, do we? Now, I must go. I need to go home and sleep. I am exhausted.'

'Do you wish to see Bandar by yourself first?' Ali asked when the surgeon had gone.

Samantha grimaced at the thought of what Bandar would say when he saw her. 'I don't know, Ali. I was feeling so happy, but now I feel sick with nerves. Bandar won't think I've come after him for his money, will he?'

Ali shook his head at her, his expression exasperated. 'Women!' he said, and took her arm in much the same way Bandar always did, brooking no nonsense and no protest. 'They can be so blind. The man is besotted with you.'

'Besotted?' she echoed as Ali steered her from the room and along the hospital corridor.

'He left you all his prized racehorses, including the favourite to win the Derby. *That* is besotted!'

CHAPTER SIXTEEN

BANDAR came back to consciousness slowly, dazedly.
He could hear things going on around him but could not
seem to open his eyes. He mumbled something and a
female voice asked him his name. He swore, and she
laughed. He eventually pried his eyelids open to see a
nurse bending over him, smiling.

'I see you've returned to the land of the living,' she said.

Bandar's foggy brain suddenly cleared. He had not
died on the operating table. He was alive!

But for how long?

'How did the operation go?' he rasped, his throat like
sandpaper.

'Very well indeed. Mr Pring got it all.'

Tears welled up in his eyes. Bandar turned his face
away so that the nurse would not see.

'Just rest,' she said, and pressed a gentle hand to
his shoulder.

He drifted off again. For how long he did not know.
When he opened his eyes he was in a different room.
And it wasn't a nurse standing by his bed but Ali,
dressed in traditional Arab robes.

'Ali?' he said, and went to lift his head. But it seemed too heavy. He groaned with the effort, then gave up.

'You should lie still,' Ali advised. 'Here. The nurse left you some ice to suck. She said you might want it.' And he popped a couple of small pieces into Bandar's mouth.

'Do not complain about my being here,' Ali went on, just as Bandar was about to. 'I will not be staying long, now that I know you are all right. That infernal coronation starts tomorrow, or I would not leave at all.'

'You cannot let your brother down,' Bandar whispered.

'The royal jet is waiting for me at Heathrow. I will be back in time.'

'Thank you for coming,' Bandar said, his friend's kindness bringing a lump to his throat.

'My pleasure. But there is someone else here far more suited than I to holding your hand and feeding you ice.'

Bandar sighed. 'You have not hired me a private nurse, have you?' It was the sort of thing Ali would do.

'No. I was speaking of your fiancée.'

'My *fiancée*?'

'Fiancée gets Samantha more rights than calling her your Australian girlfriend.'

'Samantha is here?'

'She was here when I arrived; she'd fainted dead away on the floor in the hospital foyer.'

This time Bandar's bandaged head shot up from the bed. 'She is all right?'

'Apparently she fainted when she found out you were already in Theatre. Now she is worried sick that your cynicism will make you think things that are not true. She keeps talking about your obsession with secret agendas.'

'Where is she?'

'Outside, pacing up and down the corridor. Shall I go and send her in?'

Bandar could not believe it. She was here. She had come after him.

'How did she find out about my operation?'

'Do not ask foolish questions like that. She is a woman. All you need to know is that she loves you, Bandar. Never doubt that.'

'It is hard not to doubt when you have spent a lifetime doubting. But I decided if I came through this operation I would put doubt aside where Samantha is concerned. I am going to marry her, Ali. If she will have me.'

'But you have only known each other a week,' Ali said, frowning.

'Some weeks are longer than others. Besides, when you have been to the brink of death, you realise there is no time to waste. I have made up my mind. Send her in. Then get yourself to Dubar.'

Ali nodded. 'You always were a stubborn boy. And often unwise in your choice of lady-friends. But you have picked well this time. You must come visit us in Australia when you feel up to the trip.'

'I will.'

'I presume I will have to hire myself another vet?' Ali said drily.

'I hope so.'

'You will owe me another favour.'

'When you get home you will see I have repaid you well already. There are five excellent broodmares in your stables which have not cost you a single cent.'

'Ahh, yes, I heard about them from Cleo. But I presumed *I* was up for the two million, since I was the one who told you to be generous to the Widow Higgins.'

'They are gifts, my friend.'

'In that case, I am in your debt. Till next time, Bandar…' A quick bow, a sweeping wave of his hand, and he was gone.

With Ali's departure, Bandar's heartbeat quickened, his eyes fixed on the door through which Samantha would come.

And suddenly there she was, looking terribly nervous as she came into the room and walked slowly towards his bed. She was wearing a skirt, a long flowery thing which showed off her slender figure. The top was pink, and rather low cut, definitely enhancing her natural beauty. Her face showed traces of recent weeping: her eyes were puffy and still glistening. Her hair was down, though a little messy—as it had looked that last morning, after they'd spent many hours in bed together.

'Please don't be angry at me for coming,' she choked out before he could say a word.

Bandar's heart flipped over.

Angry? He could never be angry with her. She was his life now. His future. His reason for living.

Nothing else mattered.

He reached out his hand and she came closer.

'Sit,' he said, and patted the side of his bed.

She sat.

He reached up and laid his palm against her cheek. She tilted her head into it, her eyes closing on a sigh.

'You will marry me, won't you?' he said softly.

Her head jerked up, her eyes flying open.

'No arguments now, little Love-slave. You must do as your lord and master commands.'

Samantha took his hand in hers, then shook her head at him. 'Australian girls never promise to obey their husbands, Bandar. Marriage is a partnership, made with love and respect for each other.'

Bandar smiled. She was not going to fall in with his wishes easily. But then, would he want her to?

'I don't like it when you smile like that,' she said stiffly.

'Smile like what?'

'Like you're keeping secrets from me. There are to be no more secrets between us. I will never marry a man who keeps secrets.'

'Very well. I love you, Samantha Nelson. I love everything about you, but mostly your contrariness and your courage and your character. But if you want the total truth, I did not always love you. I set out to seduce you because you were the ultimate challenge to my male ego. Plus the perfect distraction for my state of mind. Your secret agenda gave me the opportunity to have my wicked way with you without complications or consequences. I did not mean to fall in love with you. But I did.'

'I didn't mean to fall in love with you, either. You were to be just a fantasy lover. But sometimes, what is written is written.'

Bandar frowned at her. 'You have been talking to Ali.'

Her smile was slightly sheepish. 'He told me quite a lot about you while we were waiting for your operation to be over.'

He scowled. 'I will kill him.'

Samantha laughed. 'No, you won't. You owe him your life. You cannot kill him. Besides, you love him.'

'I love *you*,' he said passionately, pulling her hand over to his mouth to kiss it.

Tears rushed back into Samantha's eyes. Tears not just of happiness but wonder. He loved her. And he wanted to marry her. Which meant he trusted her.

Samantha knew it had to be incredibly hard for Bandar to trust a woman. He must truly love her.

But no more than she loved him.

She put her head down onto his chest and sighed. 'You must never leave me again,' she whispered. 'Not for a single minute.'

'Nor you me,' he returned, his hand stroking her hair. 'We will have another bed put in here till I am allowed home. And we will be married as soon as it can be arranged. Do I have to ask your father for your hand in marriage? Is that not your custom in Australia?'

The thought rather amused Samantha. She lifted her head and smiled at him. 'Yes, indeed. That is the custom in Australia.'

'Then it will be done.'

And so it was done.

Samantha would never forget the look on her father's face when Bandar asked him for her hand in marriage. The looks on her brothers' faces at their wedding were just as priceless. Ali refused to let them have some small civil service in the city. They were married at the Royal Dubar stud—the ceremony taking place in the magnificent pavilion by the pool, the reception held in a marquee which only a billionaire sheikh could afford.

Samantha listed that day as one of the happiest days of her life. Though none could really compare with the day Bandar asked her to marry him in that London hospital room. Or the day, less than two months after their wedding, that she told Ali she was pregnant. Amazingly, when she stopped taking the Pill, Samantha had no trouble conceiving at all.

Bandar had been in awe of his child growing in her belly right from the start, becoming impatient towards the end of her pregnancy to see his son. They'd known it was a boy from the ultrasound.

The joy and wonder which lit up Bandar's face when she handed him little Ali straight after the birth would remain imprinted on Samantha's memory for ever. The look of total love he'd given her was pretty memorable as well.

Oh, yes, that was the happiest day of all. For with the beginning of their family, Samantha realised that neither of them would ever be lonely again.

A Special Offer from

HARLEQUIN *Presents*

This August, purchase 6 Harlequin Presents books and get these THREE books for FREE!

ONE NIGHT WITH THE TYCOON
by Lee Wilkinson

IN THE MILLIONAIRE'S POSSESSION
by Sara Craven

THE MILLIONAIRE'S MARRIAGE CLAIM
by Lindsay Armstrong

To receive your **THREE FREE BOOKS**, send us 6 (six) proofs of purchase from August Harlequin Presents books to the addresses below.

<u>In the U.S.:</u>	<u>In Canada:</u>
Presents Free Book Offer	Presents Free Book Offer
P.O. Box 9057	P.O. Box 622
Buffalo, NY	Fort Erie, ON
14269-9057	L2A 5X3

- -

Name (PLEASE PRINT)

Address   Apt. #

City   State/Prov.   Zip/Postal Code

098 KKJ DXJN

```
Presents
Free Book
Offer
PROOF OF
PURCHASE
HPPOPAUG06
```

www.eHarlequin.com

If you enjoyed what you just read,
then we've got an offer you can't resist!

Take 2 bestselling love stories FREE!

Plus get a FREE surprise gift!